REEF MIND

HAZEL ZORN

Cover art by Becca Snow
Interior Illustrations by Echo Echo
Edited by Alex Woodroe

Content warnings are available at the end of this book. Please consult this list for any particular subject matter you may be sensitive to.

TENEBROUS

PRESS

REEF MIND © 2025 by Hazel Zorn

All rights reserved. No parts of this publication may be reproduced, distributed or transmitted in any form by any means, except for brief excerpts for the purpose of review, without the prior written consent of the owner. All inquiries should be addressed to tenebrouspress@gmail.com.

Published by Tenebrous Press.
    Visit our website at www.tenebrouspress.com.

First Printing, September 2025.

The characters and events portrayed in this work are fictitious. Any similarity to real persons, living or dead, is coincidental and not intended by the author.

Print ISBN: 978-1-959790-41-9
eBook ISBN: 978-1-959790-42-6

Cover by Becca Snow.

Interior illustrations by Echo Echo.

Edited by Alex Woodroe.

Formatting by Lori Michelle Booth.

All creators in this publication have signed an AI-free agreement. To the best of our knowledge, this publication is free from machine-generated content

Selected Works from Tenebrous Press:

Puppet's Banquet
by Valkyrie Loughcrewe

Casual
a novel by Koji A. Dae

All Your Friends are Here
stories by M.Shaw

TRVE CVLT
a novel by Michael Bettendorf

A Spectre is Haunting Greentree
a novel by Carson Winter

From the Belly
a novel by Emmett Nahil

Mouth
a novella by Joshua Hull

Lumberjack
a novella by Anthony Engebretson

Posthaste Manor
a novel by Jolie Toomajan & Carson Winter

The Black Lord
a novella by Colin Hinckley

Dehiscent
a novella by Ashley Deng

House of Rot
a novella by Danger Slater

Agony's Lodestone
a novella by Laura Keating

More titles at www.TenebrousPress.com

*For Aaron.
Your loyal friendship brought out the writer in me.
Thank you, for your encouragement.*

> "There's terrible evil in the world."
> "It comes from men," said Holly. "All other elil do what they have to and Frith moves them as he moves us. They live on the earth and they need food. Men will never rest till they've spoiled the earth and destroyed the animals."
>
> —Richard Adams, *Watership Down*

MATT

I DON'T KNOW what I'm supposed to do with you. I've never been good with children, but I have to do something. You're my fault, after all, every monstrous bit. I wonder how long it would take to break your tiny neck. Would it snap like a frail bone, or shatter? I imagine a lightning-shaped crack bisecting your face as my strong hands crush your throat. Maybe not. I've seen rocks bounce off you. Your skin is deceptively strong despite its porcelain appearance.

Your smile is a wooden thing trying to mimic flesh. The rope tether around your waist is always stretched as far as it will go. I won't let you touch me. Your little sneakers and your red jumper are strange birthmarks, like a plastic toy that's been painted, because what you grew from doesn't understand clothes.

You've stolen from me. My eyes, for instance. It's unsettling. It's not how a real father would feel. But what is particularly gruesome is your resemblance to her. The dark, wavy hair that frames your face. The shape of your lips.

You have no right.

There were so many deaths in those days. Gruesome, awful ones, too. There were no more doctors to call, no hospitals that weren't overgrown with psychedelic anemones and stalked jellyfish. I grew up with faith in social structure. There was always someone to call. A doctor, a senator, an *expert*.

Amanda was one of the last to get sick. There was talk of infection spreading before that, perhaps caused by bacteria in the ocean. We knew things were warming up, after all. I admit, living in such a beautiful place made me carefree. I retired early and was determined to relax in paradise. That was how I saw La Jolla:

paradise. There was nothing the place could do to offend me. Not even the teens and tourists overtaking the stairways to the beach, or the bum surfers, or the resorts driving up the price of housing. The sun and surf altered my brain. I used to tell Amanda it turned off the asshole in me.

Most mornings Amanda would do her nails in nothing but her sports bra and boy shorts, while the overhead fan kept the cool sea breeze circulating. I try to remember her like this, because I can't think of the way she looked at the end of it. We lived in a one-bedroom apartment above an ice cream shop with a beach view. It's overtaken now, our old place. In a way it became Amanda' casket, with the exception that people are usually dead in those.

Amanda was a good woman. She was a lifeguard in the day and a CPR instructor at night. She even taught dogs how to surf. Humans enjoy water, you see, but it can kill us. We are not made of stone. We have beating hearts, and lungs that fill with air. A big wave can overtake even the most experienced surfer and drive them to the bottom so they don't come up.

Amanda and I had a commonality. We were both burdened with the frailty of human life. We carried that constant vigilance in our postures. We met in a bar. Pretty standard, I know. She was still in her lifeguard wetsuit. I thought she looked built: all muscles and square angles. Her short height gave her a look of compressed strength. She sat next to me and ordered a real drink, top shelf whiskey without ice. My look made her laugh shyly. "I deserve this. I just saved a kid from a riptide."

I had a feeling. A good one. So, with a half shrug, I mentioned that I'd once saved an entire family from a burning building. Two kids, one an infant.

Her face froze. The little bit of cleavage that showed above the zipper of her wetsuit seemed to rise to her chin, hunched as she was over the bar. And then her mouth, those sunburned lips, quirked up. "Are you trying to one-up me?"

"Absolutely," I said, reaching into my pocket. The St. Florian medal from my firefighting days gleamed against the dark wood of the bar top. Our eyes met, sparked, then kindled with laughter. I wish I could remember that night better. It turned into early morning, our glasses empty, talking about everything.

There are a lot of people you can connect with in life and have sex with. But the desire to be exclusive only ever happens rarely. It is as if all of the good things in the world are mediated through one specific person. I didn't want to miss another moment of Amanda. She became my life.

One thing I want you to understand is that she's not your mother. You don't get to claim that. I don't care what you've mimicked, what you *stole* from us. Your kind wear our skins like a battle trophy. That's how I see it. It's kind of sick, especially considering that Amanda couldn't have children. She wanted them, though. That's what I find so difficult right now.

Would *she* want you?

I was so happy that I admit, I ignored the signs. Little things were going wrong. Odd things. And then quarantines went into effect on every coast. The National Guard shut down the highways. I was determined that I *wouldn't* leave, pretending I had a choice. I don't think the people inland would have taken me in. Only people with places to go, family to be with, tried to escape.

Some people did escape. It got so bad that parents left infected children behind in hotel rooms. Horrible people. People with no sense of duty. That wasn't me. I had EMT training. I volunteered to ride in the ambulances, because medical personnel were fleeing too.

I remember one of those children, abandoned in a bathtub on the fifth floor of a beachfront motel. He was curled up on his side with his hands crossed over his chest, fitting neatly in a square of window-shaped sunlight. The smell made its way to me first. Thick brine and urine. It scoured the inside of my throat with an unbearable itch and made me cough.

I'd stopped in the doorway and realized I dreaded approaching him. His size and his near nakedness made him more difficult to look at. He wore swim shorts decorated with colorful fish. The short arms and round fists, not quite baby-like but not completely those of a gangly child, were covered in blotches of color. Sores.

Even with the fitted mask on my face, the protective gloves, I grew anxious as I picked him up—limp, but breathing. The sores on his skin were alive. From them grew villi, waving fingerlike, turning toward me to point in judgment.

HAZEL ZORN

I told Amanda she should stop going into the water, and she laughed me off. "The water is coming to us. I don't think we can get away from it."

As La Jolla emptied of tourists in the weeks before the shutdown, we were inundated by eager marine biologists as a substitute. They got into fights with the Ecological Reserve teams, arguing that preservation didn't outweigh safety. They claimed that an unprecedented and explosive coral bloom had caused the sea level to rise. Tourist agencies tried, ridiculously, to compare our newly submerged streets to Venice.

I started to see the columns of coral slicing the skyline from our balcony. They were growing where the beach used to be. To call it rapid growth was an understatement.

It felt like an invasion. The construction of a new city, edging us out.

AMANDA

I GUESS I had a son once.

I was thinking Robert. Or Declan. Or perhaps Paul, after my grandfather. It doesn't matter. It's possible to love someone without a name. That black-and-white image of my son's little body hugging itself will never leave me. A tiny little thing with a scrunched-up face. Already exhausted by such a short life and relieved to be done with it. The sonogram tech pressed the probe into my belly, making the dead body flop sideways within that cone.

I could not bear the brunt of the absolute misery and pain all women are expected to endure. It broke me. My sob was a sharp exhalation that made my whole body contract. The fluorescent lights burned my eyes, blurred, the brightness breaking containment and overtaking the ceiling. No baby looks natural as a corpse. As I was wheeled away to surgery I suddenly understood my parents' divorce, my father's struggle with drinking. As I reflect on this now, I guess it's not strange that I met both of my husbands in bars.

I took up surfing because I think I craved self-destruction. I couldn't kill myself, but I figured I'd give Mother Nature her best shot. I know that's stupid. We're all stupid. We all think we're in control when we aren't. We say things like, *your baby got his wings in Heaven*, or *everything happens for a reason*. People want to force optimism all the time because they feel like they have to. But the only right thing is a half shrug after a finger of scotch, when the lights are low, when honesty becomes easier. That's when people finally say *fuck this*.

That's the thing about Matt. Matt didn't try to say the right thing. Matt just wanted to have fun. There was a sense of bravado about him that charmed me. The midwestern hero, I guess. He liked good beer, but nothing too fancy. He owned only a ten pack of white t-shirts and various swim trunks. He'd had two big disappointments in life that didn't cut him deep. I suppose it's because he grew up in some suburb. A place where everyone knew one another and kept the rabble away, a place that told you to check off some boxes and everything would go right in life. He was comfortable, like a soft bed I could land on after I'd lanced my boils and bled away the grief.

He positioned himself as the solution to my life's sorrows. It was arrogant in a cute way. *Depressed, baby? Try my risotto and tell me you're not better. Anxious? How about I make you a drink? Or maybe you'd like the stronger medicine between the sheets. Doctor Matt at your service!* It really was a tonic to all the hurt. I wanted to forget the country of pain I'd come from, the one that seemed to demand my citizenship. Maybe I could live the last chapter of my life in peace. Maybe I could be happy.

Maybe.

AMANDA

ONE EARLY JULY, two surfers vanished at Windansea beach and were never found.

At the time, the ocean was rolling with lackluster-to-middling surf, which meant an easy day for a lifeguard. The surfers were the only two in the water, straddling their boards, one with his hands on his hips. Their wetsuit-clad backs were black beetle shells. Doubtful they'd get a good set.

How much time passed? A few minutes. Maybe five. I had turned my back, asked an assistant to put my duffel in a locker. I know I put on sunglasses. My mind had the same feeling my eyes did when a grain of sand got in them. The sun was as hot and close as a surgery lamp. It was too quiet, maybe. I looked out over the sea, the calm but moving blue water that stretched out all the way to the horizon. There was nobody there.

I didn't know what to do. I wondered if I'd really seen those surfers at all.

The rest of the day passed by without incident. I turned away some teens who couldn't prove they knew how to surf. Pallid things, and awkward in the water. Not Californian, I was sure. The air grew cooler as the sky darkened. I donned an oversized hoodie and found a group of people passing around beers on the beach. Matt was there, happy to see me off work. The bonfire made everyone look orange.

"Did anyone else see them?" Matt asked, when I told him the story.

"Who?" asked one of my lifeguard colleagues. "Nobody went surfing today."

"How can you be sure?" Matt was defensive.

The lifeguard shook his head. "Quiet day. A few teens messed around in the shallows and that's all."

The itch was back, the one in my brain that I couldn't scratch. I shrugged. "It was an easy day."

"Babe?" Matt turned to me.

"It was a *quiet* day." I looked out to the dark ocean.

I found that I believed what I was saying.

I don't know when I saw them, but it was after the incident. The itch in my mind spread like the prickles in a limb that had fallen asleep. A group of flounder passed by my window, and then I went to the beach to see the coral towers. High as skyscrapers. Across the shore, calcium carbonate growth spread as tree roots do, long fingers digging into the sand and clutching at the ground. A drowned giant trying to pull the dry land down with him. Nobody stopped me, alone, walking into the locus of the strange invasion of our land.

I felt like something—the sand stirring, or the wind blowing—had a sense of me and my movements, observing me with inquiry. So much so that I laughed and said aloud, "what is it?" The reply was felt, like a wet cloth had been laid over the world, and all that remained was a muted and embarrassed silence. I walked on like a chastened child.

The skeletal structures were blooming, stalks growing and putting out limbs, algae colors carpeting columns and shelves. I was drawn to a field of crinoids. Their limbs waved innocently in the air. Living feather dusters. Beautiful, if I was honest. Ethereal. In the center of those flowering structures were white replicas of human faces; the same two faces repeating over and over, their eyes shut and their mouths whispering silently. It was them.

As a knee-high child, I recognized the back of my mother's legs in department stores; now here I had the same feeling. The surfers from that day. That quiet day.

Their lips were mouthing something I couldn't hear. A headache started behind my eye, a dull pain that seemed to be intensifying. I backed away from their faces and the pain receded, distance unspooling like yarn. Queasy, I ran back to our crumbling civilization.

I never told Matt where I'd been.

"He can't stay here." The boy's mouth was open in a silent scream, his eyes squeezed shut. The translucent fingers all over his skin

REEF MIND

flicked the air in agitation. "Matt," I tried again, speaking louder. "He's in pain here."

Matt was difficult for me in those days. I tolerated him and his denial of things, his inability to see the world for what it was. At that time, the hospitals were not an option. Raided, then abandoned. We'd agreed to stop going out. An agreement he'd broken, due to some sense of misplaced nobility. And now he'd brought the outside into our lives.

"I can't take him to the rec center, Amanda. Do you know what they're doing to people there?"

I did. Burning their bodies. The black smoke tainting the air with the greasy smell of melted fat and skin, making me gag. I kept my voice even. My patience was in short supply. "He can't be here. In our apartment. He—" here I stopped myself from saying *belongs*—"he should go to the beach."

He railed at me, then. Didn't I know that there was no beach anymore? It was colonized by an invading force, if anything. Really, how could I say such a thing? I may as well feed this kid to a lion. What was the matter with me? How could I *give up?* As we argued, the little boy's arms and legs thrashed in an uncanny sort of fit. His open mouth flickered, a purple light lit deep in his throat. It threw my shadow back. Matt gasped.

I didn't see him pick up the hammer. I blinked and the image changed, like a skip in a film. Now it was time for him to feel the shame he was attempting to place on me. I realized for the first time since the coral invasion—amid the not-quite present infection stirring strange thoughts in me—my husband's exhaustion: the bruised look under his eyes, the tremble of his jaw. In his eyes I saw his amazement about the world now, that everything he knew was over, after months of mystifying changes ending in this horror he'd brought into our living room.

Matt looked close to tears. His arms fell to his sides. *Do something*, he urged me. *Do something.* I heard the clatter of the hammer falling to the floor when I turned my back. I looked at the boy on the ground and felt that pain behind my eye again. Something was probing me, like a surgical instrument tentatively testing an unknown piece of meat, studying, wondering where to cut. I disguised my grimace by putting my hand over my mouth and bowing my head.

"Poor thing."

The boy's mouth opened again into a silent scream.

The pain was a rod connecting my eye to my brain then, an unheard frequency vibrating it to such intensity that my eyes watered. I clenched my fists as the fit passed in the way a set of particularly choppy waves hits a body-boarder. My entire body erupted into goosepimples.

Get away from that gross thing.

The thought was mine, from some animal part of me. The part that is disgusted by sickness, or sometimes the elderly. The part of me I push down with a robust sense of shame. I realized that I was, for some reason, afraid. And this fear was muted by the pain in my eye, dampening it. *I'm dying. I'm sick, like this kid.*

The thought had been so urgent that I looked up as if Matt had spoken. He saw the shine in my eyes and took it as grief for the boy. In that moment, I realized that Matt didn't understand me.

He didn't see the fear of a captive before him, probably hadn't figured out that I was ill. The guarded shell I'd put around myself was being gnawed away by the passenger in my mind, and I could no longer pretend to be the Amanda that Matt liked to be with. Our pursuit of a good time had avoided the requirements of true intimacy, and now, vulnerable, I had a real reason to grieve.

I wiped my tears and moved with a determination I felt compelled to. Matt only looked relieved.

The boy was light. Easy to pick up. He was still, and rested his head on my neck, below my chin. He could have been sleeping. I felt a tightness in my throat.

"It's alright, honey." I walked down the stairs to the first floor and waded into the street.

I loved when the dawn light dappled Matt's sleeping face, his closed eyes inches from my own. I rested my hand on his bare chest. *Any child of ours should have your nose, the curve of your lips.*

If I could . . .

AMANDA

I TOOK THE boy to Windansea Beach. I sung him a lullaby. It seemed the right thing to do. The villi all over him kissed at my bare skin where I held him. I set him down on a clear spot, a rock above the water. The coral wall loomed over us. I was shivering and wet.

In my mind, two images appeared: a bright-faced smiling boy with the wind of the Pacific Ocean in his hair; and the creature below with skin marred and squirming. The pain again. I pressed the heel of my hand against my eye, but one was enough to see the terrible metamorphosis of the child beside me.

The boy's bones cracked and snapped inside him, ballooning his little chest. His ribcage sprouted, popped several joints, and heaved upward of its own volition, leaving beneath it the former meat overcoat. It crab walked toward me just as the head it left behind turned and let out a raspy noise. A fragment of a small voice.

The unraveling of the boy before me destroyed the mind I had, smashing my sanity to bits. This thing replaced my love of the ocean with a vast and dark fear and a more incomprehensible silence, like a night without stars now dominated the ruin of our insect-like civilization. I put my hands in front of me—knowing full well I could not have moved to defend myself in any way.

The pain behind my eye flashed bright, and I wondered if I'd go blind. Instead, a high and barely adolescent voice spoke inside my head. It knew my name.

"You killed him," I said aloud.

An inhuman noise vibrated inside my skull in response, the bloom of pain behind my eye unbearable. I felt the reproach in it, the defensiveness.

"Necessary? How is this necessary? What are you?"

The villi all over the boy's tattered skin gave off their purple light, flexing and stirring, as if testing the air like antennae seeking purchase. There was no blood. The small remains were pale as fish meat. So too, fear drained from me; perhaps because I could no longer maintain it. I felt the probing again, the unbidden images.

I felt pity for this traveler before me, the depths of its ocean invaded, boiled, made foul.

I was made to understand what was devouring me from the inside.

Tears of fury filled my eyes. Exhausted, I lowered my forehead to the rock.

It was pitch black when I finally awoke, stiff and uncomfortable. Trembling in the cold, I looked down at my hands. My fingertips were pushed through a small skull, holding it like a bike helmet. The skin had squirmed away from him, then, leaving only this.

Purple pinpricks of light dotted the coral shelves.

Raised bumps dotted my skin. I said nothing about them to Matt, adhering to some sort of instinct I had made peace with.

We lived, in those following months after the boy, as simply as we could. I remember Matt with his head in his hands, a bottle of tequila on the ground, a black cell phone next to it. It had finally stopped working. He'd been checking it obsessively for news. Survivors. Anything. He took a drink, then looked at me with shining eyes, mourning the loss of a world he knew and trusted.

I walked over to him and wrapped my arms around his head. I let him press his forehead against my chest. At first, he was willing to sink into me as usual, until I felt him stiffen, lips parted against the side of my breast.

Horror trembled in his eyes. "Amanda?"

He saw my pebbled skin, bloodless but inflamed. They were all over my stomach. Did it hurt? I don't know. It was different, but not exactly pain. Matt fretted over me.

I sat by the window in the light and would not move, not even to eat. I stopped going to the bathroom, I guess. I didn't think of such things until Matt reminded me of them, and I grew annoyed. The bumps warmed in the light. They were tender to the touch.

In the days that followed, my skin grew fingers.

REEF MIND

Matt?
    Is he even in the room with me anymore?
    It's lonely.

MATT

I KNOW NOW that barracuda rarely pick fights they can't win.
They're still unnerving fuckers, with their dark eyes and needle-sharp teeth. Sometimes they follow me around when I'm outside, hoping we'll be predatory comrades. If I stand still, they get bored and float on. They're attracted to the glint of shiny objects because they can't see for shit.

Amanda noticed that right away. She slipped out of her bracelets—I thought she was having a fit—and tossed them. The calm of the restaurant imploded when the window shattered.

The first stupid thought I had was, *are there flying fish in La Jolla?*

I'd been fishing in the Cove and had never seen one, so it didn't seem like an altogether idiotic thought, but, the fish streaming through the window like ravenous eels had shimmering scales and teeth, and it wasn't until one of them clamped down on the golden cuff-lined arm of a teen girl and started tearing at her that we realized the danger. Three feet long, mouths like scissors. Moving through the air like it was water.

I didn't fight back. I didn't move at all. It was like watching a play. A diner with a fillet knife jumped over a downed chair, weaved around a few screaming bodies on the ground, and sliced a large fish down the side. The wound was a thread, then parting lips. The barracuda floated to the ground. Fish caught in boats gasped and struggled. But this one didn't. It didn't make any sense.

"Are you seeing this?" I asked, but Amanda didn't answer. She was tugging my arm, trying to get me to leave. It just didn't make any goddamn sense. "Look at them!" I said, louder. "They're breathing!"

REEF MIND

The air had changed. It felt thicker to me, at first. Richer. And then came the lightheadedness. It was a flood of oxygen and something else I don't understand. It shimmered in the air sometimes, like rainbows on an oil spill.

I'm told it was what helped the fish leave the water. People started passing out, and the mass exodus to higher ground started. I fit a respirator to my face, one that was programmed to filter the air and prevent hyperoxia. That was how I stayed with the EMTs until the end, pulling bodies out of shops and hotel rooms.

The problem at that point wasn't always sickness. People who passed out were preyed on by opportunistic creatures. Crablike things, carnivorous fish. They'd drag people away, out to the ocean, I think. I don't know why. I learned to use a harpoon. We all did, operating like primitives for a while as we adjusted to the new paradigm. The first guy that learned guns didn't work anymore was chewed up by a Great White. An airship with teeth raining blood and fleshy chunks on the landscape. It terrorized hikers on Torrey Pines for weeks.

The coral towers that grew from the water took over the coast. Satellites from space compared it to the Great Wall. Every beachfront was like this. Even places that hadn't seen many coral gardens at all, places where ecologists lamented we'd killed them off. The outline of every continent was slowly enclosed in a cage of calcium carbonate.

A coral invasion. That was the last thing I heard from the news. Humanity used to be so connected. We carried the world in our pockets.

We thought we knew everything.

I don't know why technology stopped working. Machinery, gadgets, appliances. All of the progress of industrialization was wiped out. Even the respirators and air filters stopped operating. Maybe that's because technology isn't alive. The coral can't use it. It manipulates the living. Invades it.

Alters it.

Like I said, Amanda got sick. We'd adapted to the lack of electricity with battery powered air filters and lamps, which would eventually run their course and die forever. I'd nailed boards over the windows. Flickering shadows sometimes eked through the slats, making spears of sunlight blink over the hardwood. I scavenged for provisions before barring the door to our apartment. I didn't think anyone would try to hurt us.

It was for me. I was afraid I'd abandon her.

I used to hate funerals, but I see now that they're cathartic. They provide a space, I guess, that says you can blubber and look the fool and nobody will give you any shit or call you weak or nuts. Loss is hard, but loss without the chance to say goodbye is worse.

When my mom died, the church she grew up in held the service. I don't remember much but the toll of the bell, the black cassock the priest wore, and the candlelight that blurred and stretched in my underwater vision. Several old women shook my hand outside, most of them wearing black lace on their heads. I think they shared condolences or told me that the world was still good.

The sky was bright blue despite my sorrow. I resented it, somehow. The months that followed were akin to a fugue state. No real memories, just the aftertaste of a long sorrow. Misery upon misery, the soft and pliable world now full of sharp edges.

Losing Amanda was worse than that.

The top of my wife's head pulsed like a newborn's soft spot for weeks, her eyes squeezed shut, her mouth stretched in a rictus of pain. I heard the papery noise before the bloodless split as her skull grew white organ pipes in a crown around her head.

When I dared to glance back at her from across the room, her head was back, her mouth slightly open, one hand resting palm up on her knee, the other covering her crotch. I took in the curve of her tanned legs, her spread open thighs. I was struck by grief, my stomach feeling the way I did when I missed a step. It curbed my arousal, made me sick with the realization that we'd never make love again.

Through the windows of Amanda' skull, fiery orange polyps wormed out. I thought that was it. I thought it was over. But she was not dead. Instead, her hands rose and pawed the air, feeling for me. "Matt?" she asked. She said my name in this way several times, but I couldn't touch her.

I wouldn't.

Newborns slide out of someone's flesh in a sandwich of blood and shit. I saw it in ambulances more than once. Life struggles and breaks through. Why is it so violent?

I was witnessing the birth of a new world in La Jolla and didn't know it. Or maybe I was in denial. I didn't ask for it or expect it. Just as I didn't ask for, or expect, a daughter.

You.

I knew people who wanted kids and couldn't have them. And people not looking for them got them. Those same people, whose hearts made room for something they didn't expect, lost those precious little lives when the coral emerged.

It's enough to make me drink, though I don't anymore. Amanda wasn't a drinker, but she did have a few when tempted to melancholy. She had trouble with children. She loved them too much. And she'd lost three herself. *A womb is often a grave. One that many people have to carry around. Isn't that fucked up?*

I learned that she'd had two miscarriages and one stillbirth. The ex-husband—I never learned his name—left. She tied her tubes. Took care of her mother, buried her, swore off love. There was no family behind her or in front of her, she often said.

"Just me myself and I until the end of the world."

"But I'm here now," I reminded her. And when she didn't answer, I added, "right, babe?"

Amanda stopped asking for me. Her long vowels turned into clipped consonants before going mute. Perhaps she gave up. Or she could no longer speak. Her throat was colonized by a wriggling invasion of fauna that cast bioluminescent shadows on the roof of her mouth. But her head turned in every direction I was, a skeletal smile that knew me and knew I was watching all of this. Her bones had grown to encase her skin, and then sprouted: Her ribs into shelves, her spine like a row of stegosaurus columns.

    I left when she began to bloom. The polyps in her eye sockets puckered at me as I broke down the door.

    Does she hate me now?

    Can she feel anything?

AMANDA

SOME PEOPLE MIGHT call pregnancy a sickness. Others take a more nuanced view. And then there's someone like me, chasing after it.

My body changed. There were physical difficulties, even pain. I accepted this with a sincerity that looked like madness to others. I know this because I was made responsible for their feelings on the matter. *Oh no, what is that?* they would say when they saw it under my skin, the conical shape of an elbow gliding from my belly button to my ribs. Perhaps they'd be startled by the lurch my midriff made on its own. *Weird,* they described it. Or *alien.*

Not as startled as I was to experience the sensation of total loss. The denial as the ache intensified up my back, the sheer horror of absent movement, the groaning of acceptance. The collapse of a dying star into blood.

Isn't there always a change to the body before it can share itself with another? Puberty before sex, sex before pregnancy. I was done sharing. Or, trying to. I thought I was done with change.

The coral sickness had me from the beginning. It was a sudden thing at first, nothing dramatic. An itch that spread and burned and then finally blossomed. A thing that just is. And with it, a me that is devastated, collapsed, as if I slipped through my own fingers.

I have mentioned before, my desire for self-destruction.

The winter waves of the Pacific Ocean could get twelve feet high. I used to wait for it, those wonderful sets, in the early morning. At five or six am, arrested by a consuming melancholy, I'd clutch a water bottle and stare into the damp fog. I almost wiped out.

I paddled out into the freezing waters, my limbs going numb, my hair plastered to my face in the damp, the fog heavy and thick over the beach I left behind. The first wave hit me hard and I rolled under it. It dragged me far, far out. I don't know how far, but enough that I wondered if I'd end up dead. I struggled to my board, gasping, and managed to kick out as the second wave came. And that one I cleared, with a manic burst of lightning speed, the saltwater burning the inside of my nose and throat. I overtook two lifeguards on jet skis. They followed me as I slowed, until, breathless, we all stopped near an alcove of rock. I remember laughing.

They scolded me and then hired me. I met Matt shortly after.

Where is Matt?

I have to find him; this devastated me. The me that is stripped down to the bones. The me that will have life from the jaws of death.

When I came to myself, by the window in our apartment, it was only to a part of myself. My neck, which could move, even without sight or sound but some *sense* that compelled me to turn. My left arm, which could feel the hardening of my skin, or lift to touch the bones of my face. My hand could feel the windowsill, my skin sensitive to the air outside. The rest of the body—numb to sensation.

I try to call for Matt again but cannot. So much of my body is annexed by a nightmare. I am a damaged glove that something works to fill from within. The pain behind my eye is gone, replaced by a wet presence that reassures me I am alone, that my husband has fled. It shares this information intending to reach my most personal center, to hurt my heart. In the way a tone of voice reveals the sly intent to insult and terrorize, the feeling I am flooded with is deliberate.

Anytime now. The certainty of the nightmare's climax is growing near. I clench my fist, mind desperate to exert my will, a flicker of a flame before a deluge. *Why me? Why that little boy? Why? Why?*

Again, that sense of teasing fear, the smug presence growing confident. Like it's savoring its meal. But it is not mere meat this thing is after, otherwise, why would my mind be intact? Matt mentioned lions—slaughter by such a beast would be more merciful than this. I am made to know my weakness. I am made to know that this thing wants me to understand everything that is happening to me.

My horror, outrage, and misery boil over in tearless agony. My head rolls back on my shoulders, my mouth open in a silent, unvocalized scream.

The fingers all over my skin strain and then drive sharp nails into my body—now suddenly, horribly full of sensation. With my soundless exhalation of ecstasy and terror they burst forth from me into thousands of wriggling children.

It didn't snow in La Jolla until the corals bloomed and spawned. Neon colors shot upwards like so many fireworks and settled, in some places, to blanket the ground in a multicolor cloak. I am in that storm. Blue and green, swarming from the window of our apartment. I see the ice cream shop below.

So many of me.

We float far, far away from the beach. The strange air helps with its supernatural buoyancy. The instinct is clear, consciousness shared but also commanding me. My personality pressed into service of the ocean's will. I am the coral's crop. My violation is the result of its anger and desire to reign supreme over lives that once dominated them.

I must find someone wounded and vulnerable. I must find that fertile soil, let the coral expand its territory, let it grow within a helpless life so that it may feed on the vividness of it.

A little girl, her hair in a nice plait. Hiking a wooded path with her parents. Refugees.

She scratches the side of her face.

Complains that her eye itches.

MATT

I TOOK A bottle of Tequila to Torrey Pines and camped out on a perch of rock overlooking what used to be the coast.

After a bout of uncontrollable weeping followed by headaches, I dropped the bottle off the edge and promised I wouldn't drink again. I could see the coral from that height, and breathe a little easier. My fishing nets caught flying fish that drifted by my perch and my harpoon warded off bigger things.

I felt like a ghost haunting the abandoned trails, the information plaques rendered useless and sad, the natural wildlife absent. Even the greenery—the cactuses and brush—had started to die. Down below, the coral choked the trees, encasing them in a white limestone shell.

In the first few weeks, I moped in my tent, wondering why I was still alive. Other survivors—not many—had the same deadened look in their eyes. We were husks of our former selves, alone and pale and wandering. The man closest to my small camp was nonverbal. Whether due to present traumas or something lifelong, I do not know. He crouched outside a small cave, protective. He was so skinny that his cheeks looked hollow. Older, too, his hair pure white and past his shoulders.

I called him Sir to be polite, and then it became his name. I never saw Sir hunt for fish, and despite my reservations, I began to speak to him. I told him my name. I asked if he needed food. His black eyes widened at the sight of my net, full of my fresh catch. The winds had been good to me that day. I sat a good distance away and set a fire up and proceeded to gut and then roast a yellowtail. Sir crawled over and snatched pieces that I cut into small bites, which I laid atop a rock like a small offering.

This became my routine. The only human contact I'd had since

Amanda . . . was taken from me. I was grateful to have something to do for someone else. I needed it. It was all to change again, after all. All joy a distraction in those days, a thing to be snatched.

The winds changed in the following weeks, and my catch grew smaller. I went to Sir, finally, in the evening as the sun started to set. All was awash in red and orange and gold. My shadow stretched long before me. I wondered if I should look for more survivors. It was common to hear voices sometimes, carried over the wind. I thought of suggesting this to my silent friend, when I realized that something was wrong.

Sir was standing in front of the cave, his eyes wide, as if I'd walked in on something inappropriate.

The shadow behind him moved, the dappled light catching the armored red shell of a gigantic crab. Sir let out a cry of fear, but his eyes were on me. I'd moved forward, harpoon in hand. I watched the old man throw himself onto the thing, clutching a red leg like a tree trunk he could barely encircle.

The flattened shelf of carapace atop the legs, what I would call the head, did not end in the protruding dark eyes typical of such a creature. Instead, the red shell possessed a soft underbelly of stretched skin, facial features marred but intact. The thin lips did not move, the eyes, wide set, were gray-green. They looked at me.

I understood then, the horror still fresh and piercing. This was someone Sir loved.

He kicked dirt at me. I dropped the harpoon. I tried to apologize, but it did not work. Sir retreated into the cave with the crab, and it was clear to me that I should not follow. Those claws could cut off my limbs, I was sure. Why tempt it?

A few days later, the cave was empty. I had scared off my only companion.

Alone. Again.

I do not know why people like me and Sir have been spared these mutations. Maybe things would be better if I'd gotten sick, too. If the coral would just take my body, then maybe I could resign myself to it all.

It is as if people like us have been chosen to suffer more.

REEF MIND

In the days and weeks that followed, I did not go out. Without Sir to distract me, all I could think of was Amanda. I tried to focus on remembering her voice.

It proved to be a mistake. That was what haunted me, especially at night. I could hear it. It was a singsong tune, the one she'd used when she was in the mood for sex. I'd wake up hard, and then remember that I was alone and in hell.

The problem was, when I dreamed, I became convinced it was her. That conviction blurred reality, and eventually I started sleepwalking. I'd leave the safety of my tent and walk the trails, and only wake up when a sharp wind would shock me. I was always headed in the direction of the beach, that coral city thriving with mutated looking things. Half-human half coral grotesqueries. Scuttling, crablike legs with human torsos. I tried not to look closely, nor did I study their industry. If I kept my head down and walked at a steady pace they took no notice. Or perhaps, no interest.

Maybe the coral was studying me the whole time. A lone survivor that it could use, somehow, to work its way into the human ecosystem more thoroughly.

I'm not proud of what I did.

It was in the evening when I was at my most vulnerable. Amanda's voice again, the sing-song tune. I was awake this time. Donning wool fisherman's slacks and thick rubber boots—to avoid the crown of thorns starfish lining the ground—I grabbed my harpoon, ready to find the mimic and kill it. I reminded myself that my wife was gone. The voice was not real. It was mocking me. It was a grotesque joke, a profane thing. My Amanda couldn't say anything at all, at the end.

I recited this litany of grievances all the way down to the place where the beach used to be, ducking under arches of interlaced limestone structures. I've always thought that corals were beautiful. Calcium carbonate skeletons teeming with life and color, huge sea fans as large as umbrellas and detailed like lace. I walked through it like a forest, the fish in the air as loud as any birds. The babbling, clicking, and sometimes low moans that sound like roars usually warn of lionfish, a danger to avoid. But that night the noises were unthreatening, as if the fish were getting out of my way.

Bellybutton pressed to my spine, I kept on with caution, not trusting the calm around me. The darkening sky lit up the coral structures with a psychedelic fluorescence, pink and green and violet light bedazzling the columns I passed and the shelves that rose like stacked plates. Emperor shrimp marched past me, living up to their name. I came to a clearing past the branching black coral, the long and spiny limbs parting to reveal the source of my wife's voice.

She was standing amid small, bush-like structures that came up to her knees, branches flat and bumpy, like a field of cauliflower. Their dome-like shapes had ridges that reminded me of the wrinkles on a human brain.

Amanda. Not-Amanda. White as a coral skeleton, and naked. Amanda if her body had been cast in a mold for a retail store mannequin. The freckles on her arms were gone. Her hair, usually curly and wild, was slicked back and stiff. Her mouth was open, singing her come-hither song. At the sight of me, her eyes glittered like marbles.

The shape of her was right, but none of the details. She didn't blink. But the curve of her hips, her breasts, the shoulders, the tip of her nose, all of it begged for closer examination. How could this be? My imagination dipped into a memory of red lace on pale skin, my lips hot against the cool flesh below her belly button. Her thighs spreading open and then clenching around me.

Not-Amanda beckoned me with her hand. A thrill went through me. *That's not your wife, you idiot.* I was already walking to her, a tightness in my pants that grew hard. She pressed into me then, her cool grip on my wrist, guiding my hand over her breast. Her skin was cold to the touch, her breath on my face like the smell of a salty wave on a hot day. The little noises she made were exactly as I remembered them, and I sunk down as if in deep seawater with her rocking against me.

At some point, I let myself believe it was her. I must have. The coral had taken her away and then given her back. That doesn't make any sense, I know. It made sense until the end, lying beside one another in post-coital satisfaction. Translucent tentacles the width of hair slithered up from the cauliflower coral bushes underneath us. I realized I could feel the prickle of their touch against my back, a few pinpricks at first that turned into a swarm of wasps. I sat up with a yelp as if from a dream. The tendrils had

REEF MIND

burrowed into my skin; I could feel their twitching even if I couldn't see them. They were all over Amanda, too, but she did not resist them. Her skin crawled, the threads writing under it, boiling it like wax. They coiled around her head, slithered down her chest—she cracked apart and dissolved into the ground. I remember her eyeball bouncing on the end of a string, her fingers twitching as they were lassoed and torn off before being gobbled up by the coral.

By then I was screaming, and I scrambled away backwards on my naked ass, and then ran barefoot all the way back to my tent.

Not before scraping up my legs to shit and fainting twice in the thick air. I caught a few nasty bruises. An outdoor circular security mirror showed me my back, which looked like it had broken out in some sort of pox. Red freckles. The sting wore off and became numb.

The coral had defeated me. I curled up in my sleeping bag and wept, finally ensnared by the monstrosity I'd tried to avoid. It was like it knew me now, had finally noticed me. Amanda's smiling skull was behind my eyelids.

MATT

I GET IT, I guess. You're here because you were able to trick me.

I tied you down because you navigate the air the way a swimmer does water. I've killed flying fish with clubs and deft harpoon shots, but I think I need to be more methodical with you. Your rocky skin will not be undone by simple coral fragging methods, I'm sure.

Your neck fits in the open V of my heavy-duty shears. I use them to press your head against a rock. Your expression remains placid. I'd love a daughter, wouldn't I? I see this thing of stone and flower, your small limbs, your curly hair. Is my blood in there, or are you bloodless and cold?

You're not a person. You're not a person and I am going to close these shears around your neck until it cracks. I have to kill you. You are a trick. A lie made material.

I'm not sorry.

Meeting you was one of the most horrific experiences of my life.

A week after Sir ran off, the wind changed, and fish were in short supply. I had to leave my tent and hunt, which I was not used to. I skipped meals. Mollusks and clams were scarce. I scrounged and crawled along the ground for anything. But someone else, I decided, had to be hunting there. And they were taking more than they needed. I packed up my tent to find a better spot, after three months of stagnation. Perhaps this was best. I hadn't heard Amanda's voice again, but leaving my camp felt, in part, like a new start.

My clothing had grown to hang from my thinning frame. My canteen was empty.

REEF MIND

The voices seemed like a hallucination at first, so it was the smell that stopped me. Cigarette smoke. No mistaking it. More voices next, all low and baritone, masculine to my ear. Military, maybe? The small of my back tightened.

"Reubens! You take last watch."

"Yessir, that perimeter is going nowhere."

To my left, noisy footsteps. Then, a young kid, clean shaven and blonde, stubbed a cigarette on a sea fan. He put his cap on and turned, and that was when he saw me.

I was made to put my hands on my head, to kneel on the ground while they surrounded me. They took my backpack, my tent. No guns on them, of course, but they had other instruments. Most of them wore fatigues and riot gear. They referred to themselves as a troop, with a chain of command, but I could not confirm that they were actual military. One of those militia groups, I think. An amalgamation of people with dreams of violent glory, reduced to more primitive structures.

The campsite was brightly lit by a large fire. The troop had cleared the area around them, the ground unnaturally bare. Their sunburned and scarred leader was only ever called "Sarge." He took my things, seeming disgusted by my lack of food. And then ordered me to work.

They were fragging corals, using hacksaws and bone cutters to remove growth. They tossed columns and shelves over the cliffside, cheering as they broke and cracked on the way down, clouds of stony dust rising in plumes. I wasn't given a mask and the work sent me into coughing fits, the dust agitating my lungs. The troop's goal was to expand their perimeter and establish a permanent camp for themselves. I was fodder for this goal. I was fed only enough to keep moving.

They'd overfished the area, as I'd suspected. Days after I was pressed into service, they complained about the smaller rations. I saw them dig up the last of their supply of fish, deep in the ground packed in salt.

The hunger gnawed at the camp.

Made people reckless.

HAZEL ZORN

I awoke very early—due to my hunger pains. The sun only an orange outline on the dark horizon. My stomach growled and clawed away at my insides. The air felt thick and hot. I got off my cot and realized that someone was cooking, the heat of a fire sending up blurry waves that distorted the landscape. The smell of something roasting brought beads of saliva to my tongue. A sweet aroma, something meaty, juicy. *Lobster?*

Like a man in a dream, I stumbled through the camp to the source, feeling weak and wisp-thin. It wasn't lobster, but my nose was close. Crab meat. Nearest me, three men were stooped over one large and red leg. They'd cracked open the shell and were scooping out the shiny white meat. There was so much of it that they weren't paying attention to rations. I crawled over like an animal approaching a trough. The first bites were rich and sweet. My hands became slick with grease.

Someone made a joke about the lack of lemons and butter. Laughter rippled, going on and on, reaching hysterical notes, until I realized that someone was actually screaming. I did not recognize the voice. There was no way I could have, you understand. It sent the blood from my face. There I was, a hunk of meat wadded in my cheek, looking across the feeding hordes, the fire, the spits roasting crab legs, to a thin old man with tied hands. Howling at the sky.

I spat. Gagged.

"Somebody shut him up," one of the men said.

I weaved around bodies and landed on my knees when I got past the fire. Tears blurred my eyes. "Sir? Sir?" I took his shoulders, but he twisted from me, body contorted in agony.

I blubbered. I told him I was sorry, so sorry. I wished I could vomit. I wished I were dead.

On my knees, I lowered my forehead to the ground. Sir's howling continued.

A pair of boots stopped by my ear. I looked up at Reubens, chewing at a piece of crabmeat stuck to the end of his large bowie knife. "You know this nut?" He nudged me with the side of his foot when I didn't answer right away.

"I think we're eating a person." I said. Then, in case he didn't hear: "This crab isn't what it seems."

Reubens licked his fingers, holstered his knife. "Tastes like a crab. No 'seeming' about it."

REEF MIND

"It's a person," I insisted.

"Not anymore it isn't. You ate some too, fireman. Don't be so high and mighty."

My mouth was a silent 'o' of shock. Reubens moved forward and swung his leg. His boot landed right in Sir's middle. The old man's voice choked off after an abrupt exhalation. I started forward and was overcome with light-headedness, my strength and agility sapped by hunger. My eyes blurred again. I started to crawl forward when I saw Reubens plunge his bowie knife at Sir's chest.

The knife's point made a strange noise; like a woodpecker beak hitting oak. I saw Reubens flinch, and then he took hold of Sir's arm and pulled him forward, inspecting. His teeth bared in some sort of amused realization. "Look at that." I couldn't see anything. I struggled to my feet as three men from the troop answered Reuben's summons. They made disconcerted noises.

"What is that?"

"What's happening to him?"

"It's mighty convenient." Reubens said. "You, get the rope! Secure legs and arms, I think. Don't want him crawling off."

I only stood there, confused and outraged, my heartbeat in my ears. They tied Sir down so that he could not wander away. When the men were done they went back to their duties, to feasting by the fire. I dared to creep forward after and noticed that Reubens didn't seem to mind. His eyes glinted, as if in on a joke.

Sir's belly was bright red. I assumed a terrible sunburn until I got closer. The morning light shone off it like armor. Shell. It was hardened shell. His fleshy arms ended in clawlike appendages, fingers fused together with the thumbs separate. They looked flaccid, tender. His head was bent to the ground, not looking at me. I began to shake.

Reubens called to me: "We'll be eating good for a while."

I tried not to eat. But I eventually did. I had to. There was nothing. Nothing at all edible, and no other creatures near the camp. I considered running away, but my weakness made me dependent. I doubted I'd have made it a few miles before passing out. The human body can't move without calories. They meant to work me to death, I think.

HAZEL ZORN

The shell of the crab had been dismantled and the parts propped on a rock, a macabre battle trophy. The troop had cleaned it out, rationing the rest of the meat.

Sir changed a little bit every day. He never acknowledged me, but I sat by him anyway as his eyes grew further apart and his lips stretched thin and shut. He had always been nonverbal, but the sense I had of his silence changed after a few weeks. Instead of intelligent curiosity a dumb apathy replaced him. I could no longer sit there. I could no longer think about it.

Day after day passed. I tied a cloth around my nose and mouth and set to fragging coral growths with the men.

I took the rations.

I wish I'd had the courage to die instead.

MATT

I KNOW NOW why I am alive. I didn't then, because I did not consider the premeditation involved. Can stone think? Do the tectonic shifts of the earth act with any purpose? I couldn't answer in the negative, not honestly.

But now I understand that there were forces at work.

After a few weeks, Reubens did something that changed the camp forever. He was accompanied by a small child that only came up to his waist. My heart throbbed with anxiety, until I noticed that something was odd about that child.

About you.

Reubens showed you off to the troop like you were a doll. When you turned full circle your eyes landed on me, and I saw Amanda in you. My guts clenched with recognition, the hair on my arms stood up. I was afraid that everyone would recognize you, would know my shame.

Reubens ground the lit end of his cigarette on your shoulder. It didn't leave a mark, and you didn't react at all.

He found you growing from a field of cauliflower corals. Your eyes were open, and you seemed harmless, he explained, wiping his bowie knife on his pantleg. Described you as "damned-indestructible." The troop had seen coral growth in the shape of human faces. Never a fully grown human form.

Amanda's appearance to me must have been unusual. The dark possibilities frightened me. Why only me? Was something horrible in store? The coral, I decided, must be somewhat intelligent. It targeted me, I realized. For what purpose?

You looked at me as if in answer, eyes slightly recessed in the way a sculpture is carved, the shadows giving your gaze an ominous feel.

The troop eventually decided that they didn't like you. I agreed with them; I wanted them to get rid of you. They examined you, lifted your arms, knocked their knuckles against your sheen of hair. One of them examined what looked like your clothes—to discover that there were no seams, no way to remove them. Sarge and Reubens decided to keep you around 'for observance.'

"If the coral wants to communicate, why can't she talk?" Sarge's voice was gravelly, the smell of cigarette smoke wafting over him in the thick air. The men often discussed issues at night around the fire, while I prepared for sleep.

"Not she, *it*. And it's not intelligent at all." Someone replied. "It's like those bugs that mimic birds."

"That's a possibility. A nice defensive tactic. We won't hurt it if it looks like one of our children."

"I don't think it's going to stay all innocent-looking, Sarge. What if it attacks?"

Sarge remained quiet, the glint of the fire in the one eye that was looking at me. For some reason fear replaced my blood, and my whole body tensed.

"Fireman," he said softly. "It would be wise of you to share any insight into this issue."

He asked because you were my silent shadow. It amused everyone at first, the way you stood by me when I slept, the way you followed me in the day. I'd tried to shoo you away but refused to speak to you lest I be found out. I wanted to grip the sides of your head and ask you why you were doing this to me. The swell of grief in my chest returned because thoughts of Amanda confronted me with your arrival.

"I know nothing. I want it gone."

There were a few grunts of assent around the fire at this, and I felt a weird camaraderie toward my captors in that moment. Sarge only took a long drag from his cigarette, a disembodied orange sun in the dark, rising and setting in front of his face.

"It's imprinted on you like a duckling. I want to know why."

"I don't like it." I insisted. "I did nothing to deserve this." I pointed at Reubens. "*He* brought it here, not me."

"Maybe it thinks you're safe. The noble rescue worker."

REEF MIND

Reubens replied. There were appreciative chuckles. "You're easy to take advantage of. I say we let this take its course. We're not the ones the thing is obsessed with."

Sarge didn't say anything, but his shadow bobbed in a nod.

The rarest pine in North America, the Torrey Pine, was no more. Bark was overgrown with coral anemones, some pulsing in the light of the day. Bulbous cankers replaced the needles, giving me the impression that the branches were covered in barnacles. The majestic wilderness that I used to take refuge in was now fecund and infected.

You followed me down every path I took, no matter how far I went from the camp. I hoped to lose you in an expedition that would cross several broken cliffs. Torrey Pines was known for its large cliffs, ravines, and sandstone structures. The calcium carbonate encasing everything seemed to be leaving the rocks alone. We had no explanation for it, but the troop was considering moving camp to the one place the coral hadn't touched. So, I figured, what chance did you have? Maybe I could shake you off. I imagined your tiny doll-body breaking and crashing down the rock like glass.

Our party packed up and scouted out at dawn: myself, Reubens, and three others with tools and rations. You were never far behind me. A school of jellyfish arced like a rainbow above us, their psychedelic coloring sending a spectrum of marbled light on our pathway.

"Walk slow, those things can sting." Bash, a short man with a moustache, had spoken behind me.

I looked up. They were large, their ribbon-tails innocent and beautiful in their undulations. One of them had a head so big I was sure I could sit on it. They didn't bother us, and soon they were floating away with the air currents.

The wind picked up midway through our journey. We had not seen the end of jellyfish. In the distance, headed right toward us, was a swarm. It was so dense that I thought I was looking at a gelatinous cloud. The jellyfish heads were pulsing parachutes netted together by their long stinging tentacles, which dragged along the surface of the cliffs.

"Get down!" Reubens shouted.

We scrambled. The air grew charged, reminding me of approaching lightning strikes during thunderstorms. I bolted. I maintained a sprint, hoping I could stay ahead of them. The swarm was due to pass over the cliff if the breeze didn't change. I imagined myself like an ant avoiding a broom, running along in line with the bristles until clearing the edge of them as it touched down.

The men who followed Reubens' advice were climbing down the rock. I heard their screams, followed by the crashing and booming echoes of rockfall. I did not turn back to look. In my peripheral vision I saw the psychedelic tentacles, like strings of billowing lace. The writhing curtain swept over the rocks. I felt the lash of a whip on my ankle as I cleared the swarm, a prickle that bloomed into a painful burn. Grimacing I kept on, leg throbbing with the effort. I'd reached the edge of the rock's surface.

I turned then, breathing hard. Reubens was stopped a few paces behind me, bent over with his hands on his knees, wheezing. Angry red lines marked up his pale arms. His body could not contain the tremors sweeping over him, and his eyes bulged with fear. I saw humanity in him, long disguised.

The jellyfish cleared the cliff, tentacles dragging off the edge of the rock and then dangling gracefully as they drifted on. They passed over you, bumping against you like a beaded curtain. You sat with your legs crossed, unperturbed. No stings marred your alabaster complexion.

In a miserable heap next to you lay one of our men. His sores had erupted into pustules, his mouth yawning in a silent scream. His body was so swollen he looked inflated; his eyelids balloons. As we approached him I was sure he was dead. Reubens cursed under his breath. I watched him take out one epi-pen from our small medkit and waste it on the corpse. I couldn't fault him for such a useless action. He likely felt the need to do something. Anything.

You only looked at me.

We heard grunts over the cliff's edge. Bash. He'd managed to climb down and hang on for dear life. "Barron is gone," he gasped out, once Reubens and I pulled him the rest of the way up. "Slipped when the swarm started to pass over. Just got spooked." He was trembling as well.

REEF MIND

Our party reduced, then, from six to four. Myself, you, Reubens and Bash.

Reubens whirled on you. He put both hands on the side of your head. "Not a mark on this thing," he growled. "Just watching us all get maimed? Huh? You little *freak*."

I saw his torso twist in a lunging motion, from my position behind him. I let out an exclamation when your small body went sailing over the cliffside. I do not believe that I was concerned for your wellbeing. But Rueben's capacity for brutality always shocked me.

You arced upward and then . . . twisted, like a fish.

We all watched you walk across empty space to another cliff rock. It was a startling and uncanny moment, your tiny form in the air like that, moving in this new world with ease while we felt so vulnerable and unmoored.

You touched down. Then, you turned and walked back toward us, the air shimmering like rainbows under your feet. You acted as if nothing had happened. You took your place beside me.

"What the fuck?" Bash breathed. "Reubens come on, man. We can't have this thing with us."

Reuben's complexion flashed from sickly white to mottled purple. He took out a wrench from his bag, weighed it in his hand. He looked at you. I took a step back, anticipating his swing. Maybe he'd bash your head in, see how strong you really were. And then his eyes flit to me, and his face warmed to its usual color.

"You," he said. "You tie this thing down and you try to kill it."

"What?" I blinked rapidly. "You want me to—?"

"Yeah," Bash nodded. "Yeah, that's a good idea. If it's got a defense mechanism then the fireman can take the heat." He spit pink phlegm and wiped bloody crust from his nose.

A bag of fragging tools landed by my feet.

"Go on, Fireman. We'll climb down to a nice spot. You get to work. If you wimp out we won't be sharing rations."

We climbed down the cliffside to a wide and flat shelf that arced around the cliff, the lower elevation an adjustment. I felt slightly lightheaded. Bash and Reubens set up a camp and sent me walking. They didn't want to witness it, I guess. They started to roast crab meat over the fire to incentivize me.

HAZEL ZORN

I found I did not need to be threatened. I looked down at you and found myself capable of imagining your end.

You just followed me.

My arm muscles bulge with my efforts, the steel shears cut slightly into the sides of your neck before tremoring to a halt. I hate you. I hate how you look like her. I hate how you remind me of my weakness. My grief for Amanda was exploited and now takes your tiny form and haunts me, mocks me.

My anger flares white, a new dimension of pain. My eyes swim. I wish I could shoot you, blow your head clean off and paint the rocks with whatever the fuck is inside there.

The shears clatter to the ground. Why can't I do it? I'm a fireman that's broken down doors and hacked away obstructions to save lives. I can carry two people out of a building at the same time. Why are you stronger than me? Your neck only has small lines etched into it, mere scrapes. You really are like a rock. I upend the bag for other tools. The chisel, the hacksaw. Something in here *has to* work.

I look at your face. You're watching. Are you amused? I have never seen an emotion on your face. You do not seem made to express anything. But your arm lifts, your finger points. I follow it with my eyes.

To the hacksaw.

I watch you lower yourself to your knees. The tether on your waist falls slack. You bend down. Rest your head on a small rock like a pillow.

You point again to the hacksaw, just as the sun begins to set.

I am growing cold.

FIN PART 1

AMANDA

I JUST WANTED a family. Doesn't that sound so innocent?

Behind every desire is a cold reality. It watches, smirks. Probes at any hypocrisy. It moves under what I consider to be my skin and makes me realize that I condone pain. That is what life is, after all. Pain is the only guarantee. To desire a child is to perpetuate this pain.

How then, can I blame the coral for what it has done?

There is no *me* anymore, but I still think of the child as *mine*.

This is possible, because of Matt. He must be understood, the way *I* was understood and exploited. There is no *I* in the reef mind. It wonders: What is more predictable than the human tendency toward violence? But the human trait of individuality must not be underestimated. Some universal observations are not entirely incorrect. Humans will take the easy way out. The impulsive, destructive way for the sake of an immediate result.

Matt sits on a bar stool, hunched over an amber glass with his Amanda-wife. He is recounting details from his upbringing. Amanda's eyes widen, and her mouth opens. She raises her own glass to her lips, finishes the contents, and motions for another to the barkeep.

Matt says, "lots of parents do it, Amanda."

"Is that so?" The tone of her voice suggests that she believes no such thing.

"Yes," Matt frowns at his own glass.

"My dad beat me to keep me in line." He keeps on. "Parenting is difficult. Sometimes a father has to make hard choices to steer a kid in the right direction."

REEF MIND

The Amanda-wife is quiet for a long while. Perhaps she wonders if this man she loves would be different without the beatings. Better or worse?
Her shoulders hunch.

MATT

IT WAS MORNING of the following day. From our vantage point, the sun outlined the rock around us in angry red before bursting over the edge to paint the ground with bright light. Bash and Reubens turned over the ash of the previous night's fire. The wind carried with it the smell of ocean water and fish.

Supine, my neck stiff from a night spent on the rock, I looked at the sky until the light stung. Tears leaked from the corners of my eyes and filled my ears. I blinked, my mind retreating from a hazy nightmare as the real world came into sharper focus. When I sat up, the particulars fell away like cobwebs brushed off a windowpane. But impressions and feelings remained. A thought came unbidden to me, in Amanda's voice. A memory of a warm morning, her hand on my chest. *Any child of ours should have your nose . . .*

I swallowed past the lump in my throat. I kept thinking of my father, and my own childhood. My respectful posture. My litany of "yes sir" and "no sir." His hand striking me and then embracing me warmly, proud of my accomplishments. He made me the man that I was.

Parents have a hard job.

I'd left your body behind, within a ring of powdery white dust, next to the dulled hacksaw. I'd brought back your head. I'd brought it back to prove I'd done it.

My hands trembled.

Reubens looked at your head, perched in the center of camp. Light as a bowl, sort of porous. No blood poured from the stump of your neck. Your eyes were closed. I did not know if Reubens was impressed by my deed or if he distrusted it. I could not blame him for that if so, as the two hearts within me were also conflicted.

REEF MIND

Traces of determination, parental duty, leave an after-image in my mind. The prickle along my back flares up like an angry rash whenever I doubt myself, whenever I think I might collapse. I scratch absently at my skin.

Sometimes a man has to make hard choices, my father said, taking off his belt. What kind of father would I be if I didn't whip you into shape?

I flinched. I caught Reubens staring at me, as if seeing something unexpected. Perhaps he had hoped to dispatch me, thinking I wouldn't have the guts. Or maybe he envied me, the violence I'd done to you.

"She didn't make a sound," I said to Reubens. He looked down, as if annoyed he was caught staring at you. I went on justifying myself: "It likely is a mimic of some sort. We're better off without her around."

I spoke with such confidence that the burn on my back abated. What was I becoming?

Who was I, without a purpose I understood?

"Agreed." Bash spoke, surprising me. He shouldered his pack. "I don't want to stay here. The question is, do we go on or should we head back to camp?"

Reubens shook his head. "I told Sarge we'd find a path forward. I will only concede if we cannot find a natural food source in the next day."

We bustled around with practical work, the other two moving quicker. I packed up, avoiding your head until the end. I didn't know if I should leave you or toss you over the cliff.

I picked you up and something uncoiled under the stump of your neck, umbilical in its swing. It looked like a mangled, exposed tree-root. But pulsing. *Wet*. It expanded and contracted like breathing lungs. It took a moment for my mind to recognize a trunk-like torso, the offshoots in the place of arms and legs.

I froze there, heart in my ears. *What the fuck?*

Behind me: "Fireman. Toss it. Let's go."

I felt my shoulders stiffen. I put you down instead, under a slight overhang of rock in the shade. There had been no nightmare. I felt a compulsion and I'd done it. I'd moved the hacksaw back and forth over your small neck, jostling your head from side to side. Me. I'd done it. The pain in my palms remembered, as did the muscles of my upper body.

Something in my thoughts halted as I reckoned with this. A decision.

Mine?

No.

I turned around casually. "I'll leave her there as a path marker. Just in case."

Reubens just shrugged.

I was sure you opened your eyes as I turned away. I felt them on my back, the sores lining my skin stinging in response. My thoughts were with my father again.

Sometimes you gotta break an egg so a chick can fly.

The sun was high. The rock we traversed was barren and exposed. My arms itched with the start of a sunburn.

Bash became agitated. He scratched at his own reddening forearms. "Do you think it knows things?"

I stopped and looked out over the horizon, thinking he'd spotted the approach of something dangerous. Nothing but clear blue sky. Completely cloudless.

"The coral, I mean," Bash explained. "Doesn't it seem smart?"

"It's a thing. What can a *thing* possibly know?" Reubens snapped.

"What about you, fireman? Does it seem intelligent to you?"

"What are you on about?" Reubens huffed. "Is a weed intelligent? Is cancer? Get your head out of your ass, Bash."

I had never considered the earth I lived on to be a separate organism. It was a stage prop, a setting. A nice one, sure, but nothing to think too deeply on. I saw the coral reef the same way, just one part of the background on the vast tapestry of life. But Bash made me consider it, and you, in a different way. You weren't like an animal or a plant. You could have stepped off a UFO. An alien, either to destroy all of us or to negotiate terms.

"Maybe," I finally said. "But it doesn't like us. We're like ants, and the dirt we walk on is the enemy."

"See? Yeah. That's what I think." Bash talked fast. He peeled dead skin off his arm, let it flutter in the air like leaves. "Did you ever try to talk to that coral girl, fireman? Do you think she was our chance?"

REEF MIND

I felt a coldness erupt all over my skin. If the coral could send ambassadors, were you connected to a vast consciousness? The olive branch? But no, it was not that simple, not at all. The sun was getting to me, was what I thought. And to Bash. I thought of you kneeling down. Motioning to the hacksaw. Like you wanted it, like I'd done you a favor.

"She never spoke," I explained. "You're overthinking it."

"Finally, some sanity." Reubens called back to us. "It's kill or be killed, Bash. That's always been the story. That's the human struggle. Don't fail us now."

And yet, we were failing. We walked and walked and found nothing. Reubens wouldn't stop.

Bash trailed behind me. Real slow.

The sun grew hotter before it started to set. The prickling, itching sensation on my back burned. I asked if we could rest. The light was violet, our shadows dancing blue on the rock. The heat was held in the stone, making me feel like we walked on cooking coals.

Reubens turned around to look at me, his face contorted with rage. "Bash!"

Behind me, several yards back, was a crumpled figure. I wondered about heat stroke; when was the last time Bash had asked for the canteen? And then I saw that his sunburn had a crustacean sheen in the light, and I felt a burgeoning sadness within my belly.

"Get up!" Reubens shouted. He broke into a jog and then kicked bash in the ribs. The fabric flew up. Small nubs of skin protruded from Bash's ribs, the start of jointed legs. As he rolled to his side, I saw his hands, how the fingers formed one clawed appendage with a thumb. I felt a sob rise to my throat. Reubens kicked him again. I saw too late that he meant to kick Bash off the side of the cliff.

"Stop!" I could only think of poor Sir. Reubens had blood in his eyes.

I dropped to my knees as Bash went over, the fall of rock echoing loudly. The setting sun flashed bright in my face, blinding me temporarily. Reubens was yelling. Perhaps he would kill me, too. As the spots in my vision blinked away, I realized that something was approaching.

It was you. You were walking toward us, taking our exact path. How long, I wondered, had you been tailing us?

Your body was the same limestone-rigid mannequin, the neck ending in sharp points of sawed off wood. But there was a newly grown head. It was bright red and shone like fresh blood that did not leak, a droplet that had shape and viscosity, with facial features and a moving neck. Your hair was moving, branching up from your head like jellyfish tentacles. Small orbs glowed, a phosphorescent effect from the sunlight.

Your cool fingers brushed against my shoulder as you passed me. Reubens stopped. I saw the flash of a bowie knife in the light. A deep fear pulsed through my brain. The air had shifted. Thick. *Greasy*.

Sudden shadows fell over the rock. In my mind, I expected to see hot air balloons, perhaps a zeppelin. But this, I had no context for. I had never seen such creatures in my life, nor in the ocean. I was mesmerized. At that point, I had not realized that the ocean's horrors were only beginning to surface.

Two transparent, coiled bubbles propelled through the air, shimmering in the sunlight. Like giant snail shells. They were larger than cars. They cast rainbows on the ground like glass prisms. I watched one bounce off a rock and head right for Reuebens.

Your expression was an unblinking mask of calm as the grisly event unfolded. Reuben's head was tilted up, eyes wide, as the thing gracefully descended right down onto him. I expected, for some reason, the pop of a soapy bubble, or for it to bounce. But it was like a sieve.

Lines appeared on his forehead, thin and crisscrossed. He opened his mouth. A sound like someone slurping pudding came out. Blood fountained from his throat. Teeth rained out of his mouth. The bubble ensconced his whole head with a lurch. And then his face sloughed off like a rubber mask. As the bubble descended, it filled with the red wash of blood. A splatter at first, and then a storm as it moved to disrobe the rest of his body. If Reubens was screaming, I couldn't hear it. His legs, visible

REEF MIND

underneath the lowering bubble, spasmed before they were engulfed.

My vision blurred. Tears ran runnels down my face. I was on my knees, crawling, helpless. The view below and the sprawl of the landscape gave me a sudden sense of vertigo, of complete and total helplessness. The second spiral thing, this balloon-like creature, sailed over me as if it didn't notice me at all.

I covered my ears against the gruesome noises. I wasn't brave enough to jump. The creature that had swallowed Reubens looked like a bloody water balloon. It floated lower to the rock, sloshing. I felt my stomach turn over; I burped. Something clattered next to me, a hail of bones. A jawbone, dry, skittered over to me and then bounced off my knee before coming to a stop.

Rigid, paralyzed by fear and disgust, I started to shake.

You. Your hand.

Your fingers were hard, but gentle as they stroked my hair. I dared to look up. Your mouth opened. Something strange happened, a white-hot flash in my brain. The creatures, the sea butterflies—I now knew the name for these coiled things—would not hurt me. Your language was not heard by my ears, but I understood. The butterflies cleared the area of scrap, of useless things. Filtering out what wasn't nutritious to them.

I looked at Reuben's jawbone.

I bolted up and ran. I could not help myself. You could have caught up with me, as my footing was clumsy. I climbed down a shelf, and then another, slipping and scraping my bare arms and sending the clatter of rockfall below. I wish I had not understood anything.

Parents are violent to children, to make them grow.

When I reached flat ground, the sky rotated above me. I dry heaved before blacking out in the dirt.

MATT

I WOKE UP ONCE, hungry, my tongue dry. It was dark and cold. I noticed the absence of insect noise and pulled my knees to my chest.

Dawn light slipped through the creases of my eyelids. Water droplets plopped onto the side of my head, rolling down to my nose and lips. But the sky was clear. Something blocked the sun. A pair of knees. Someone was kneeling on the ground, looking down at me. A canteen was set down.

A woman's voice said, "Hello Matt."

When I woke again it was dim out. There was a blanket draped over my body and something soft rested under my head. The wind carried with it the smell of brine. I realized I was disappointed to be conscious. But there would be no more sleep. My belly groaned.

I sat up to find myself in the shadow of a small trailer. It read, NATIONAL MARINE SACTUARY FOUNDATION in fluorescent letters across the white backdrop. Something about that made me want to laugh. I must have made some exclamation, because that was when Miriam walked into view. She introduced herself at some point, but I'm fuzzy on the details.

Short, wiry, dark-skinned. She was dressed like a gardener. She held a pair of fragging shears in her gloved hands, and a bandanna covered the top of her head. Her large-rimmed glasses, and her grey braids, made me think of a nurturing, grandmotherly figure. This was not what I said to her. In fact, I was rude.

"Who the hell are you supposed to be?"

REEF MIND

Her voice was calm in answer. "I'm part of the Coral Restoration Foundation."

"Oh. Congratulations. I think it worked." I laughed loudly, lightheaded.

Miriam sat down next to me, unruffled by my behavior. She prepared a plate of dried fruit, salted nuts, and cooked fish. She sat patiently cleaning her coral fragging tools while I ate. A full stomach made me feel more human, made my brain feel less stretched and achy. I didn't recognize where we were, exactly, as the landscape was flat and desert-like. A few pine trees in the distance were struggling against an outbreak of limestone; coral pipes had grown on one and I swore I saw a small polyp pop out and then retreat back inside.

"How did you know my name?" I asked her.

Miriam looked up then. "Your daughter told me."

"My—?" I had to swallow against the dryness in my throat. "Right."

She smiled then, and not unkindly. "The paradigm has shifted. It took me a while to adjust, too."

I looked at her tools. "I removed several growths in the mountains. They just come back. Have you had any progress?"

Her eyes shone then, her old face crinkling with well-trod smile-lines. "I'm not trying to kill the coral, Matt."

We walked around the trailer and I saw what can only be described as a garden. Stony corals were planted in rows and clearly cared for. Algae blooms colored several, but others were bare and waiting to be colonized. Miriam's supplies were in buckets: coral gum to affix growths to rock, several cutting and sawing tools for pruning and fragging. Flanking them like bushes were soft corals of a bright and psychedelic pink, their limbs moving with the slight wind, their branching structure similar to a plant I might recognize, but their blooms fleshier and rubberier. *Gorgonians*, she called them, and then talked about how easy they were to feed. It was as if we were in the suburbs and she was giving me a tour of the plants lining her walk.

It all started to feel normal. For a moment, it was as if this was someone else's dream and I was being drafted into it. Miriam smiled at me, and I mirrored it, trapped. I did not know if I was afraid. Confused, certainly. Something kept the fear down, like my senses were dampened.

I asked: "Where is my daughter, then?" This was the first time I acknowledged you.

Miriam waved toward her trailer.

Her trailer was called a "coral bus" by her former—deceased—colleagues. Their mission, in partnership with several universities, was to transport lab-grown corals in the bus to ensure their survival before planting them in their natural habitat. It was a mission of restoration, she explained. "I traveled from Hawai'i to be here, after applying for the research mission. The university where I taught agreed to put me on sabbatical." She laughed. "Isn't that funny to talk about now? Sabbatical?" She laughed again.

Miriam was committed to helping restore balance to the ecosystem. I found I admired that.

Before you came to be, when the world was dominated by my kind, there was a crisis. Algae bloom death caused by rising temperatures killed off corals, an essential part of our ecosystem. I understand that it upset the balance of life on Earth, a balance that human beings needed to live comfortably.

I see now, why she was chosen. But more on that later.

Inside the coral bus were more tools and supplies, with rows and rows of shelves containing a coral nursery. The generator had broken long ago, and the temperature was no longer regulated. You were inside, sitting on a bench in the back. Your blood red head turned toward me, but you were resting and gave me no other attention. Puzzled, I stared at you for a long time.

"She had to grow an entire head in a day," Miriam explained. "Let her rest, dad." Her hand on my shoulder prompted me to follow her outside again, into the sunshine.

"I cut off her head," I blurted out, like a child caught in a misdeed.

Miriam smiled warmly and offered her canteen. "Of course."

Again, the buzzing volume of urgency in my head felt as if it were being deliberately turned down. I looked out over Miriam's coral garden and focused on a particularly large and yellow soft coral fan. It looked like it had been cast in gold.

It wasn't that I was able to understand Miriam, so much as see what she was communicating. I found myself standing in the dirt one minute before staring out at the Pacific. I was transported to

REEF MIND

the view Amanda had, that day on the beach. How she had insisted on her quiet, uneventful day.

There were two surfers, Matt. She pointed and—

—A small boat branded as a research vessel cut through the water in broad daylight. Two surfers straddling their boards saw it, waved. The woman aboard opened a cooler and dumped something into the ocean. It's Miriam. Her hair is as white as bleached coral. Something with thick tentacles is squirming, splashing. It starfish-stretches under the boat, grows, limbs branching out from the center in a snowflake pattern. Miles and miles below, deep-sea corals ejaculate in response, a storm that rains up to foam and bubble the water's surface as the surfers are pulled under in silence—

I flinched, lightheaded. "Where did you say you were from, again?"

Miriam took her time before answering. "Hawai'i. I came to UC San Diego to study California's deep-sea corals. They grow on the continental shelves and canyons in your part of the Pacific. We'd seen unprecedented coral growth around the world, so I was curious to investigate your coast."

I opened my mouth and then frowned with the sudden onset of a headache. The sensation came back, the seeing behind the words being said.

—Thick rivers of blood drained from an old man's body as his bones encased him, growing out of precise slits, his mouth open, the sunlight plucking up the algae bloom lining his throat. The tiger sharks deposited him in the water and sailed away on the air for their next victim. He drifted down, down, down until his bones settled on the start of a fringing reef encircling an atoll. The coral ring of human bones grew and bloomed, forming at a record pace, meeting their deep-sea comrades below and then reaching up, up, up—

I felt sick. Miriam.

Miriam did something.

I open my eyes. The water is everywhere, vast and blue. A chain of islands can be seen in the distance. This is Hawai'i. Miriam's family crossed these waters from the Philippines, and she remembers the stories her grandfather told about the journey. She'd sit in the field while he worked in his large-brimmed hat, and he'd tell her about their ancestors. About how the boat was so small it was like being aboard a splinter in a swimming pool.

The coral is everywhere, too. Under the water, it stretches in all directions. A pulsing brain growing larger and larger still. And there are people down there now, thousands and thousands. I cannot tell how many. They all open their mouths to speak with one voice, bubbles pouring out of the open lips. Miriam dives into the water. Her scuba suit is branded with official university logos. She goes deep, deep down into the dark water, and I see her approach the faces. She inspects them, both of her hands caressing one, then another, looking.

Looking.

She lingers, and so do I. Her grandfather's face but cast in limestone. A sea fan imitates his gardening hat. She shoves a crowbar into his eye socket, and the shell cracks, a fissure bisecting the face. Something dark pools out of the crack, congeals, writhes. It bleeds black and squirming, fingers grasping to birth itself from his head.

I clapped my hands over my ears. Stop.

The dirt and Torrey pine-dotted landscape of La Jolla rushed back into view. I panted a bit, as if I had actually been underwater. A lightheaded feeling washed over me. Miriam stood next to me, as if we'd only been admiring her garden. My shirt stuck to my skin.

I remembered my phone in my hand, bright and brimming with information, before the internet went down. Hawai'i went first. Nobody could get out. The last flights from there were when? I couldn't remember the timeline. I was reading articles when Amanda showed the first signs of getting sick. Terms like "heterotopic ossification" scrolled past my fingertips. How did I forget?

The sun felt uncomfortably close. The skin on my back itched. I did not want to acknowledge what was happening, the dream I was partaking in. The dream that was not mine. I forced myself to talk. I forced myself to behave as if I was not having visions. "Right. So you joined Scripps. Sabbatical. Spent time on a research vessel deck crew."

Miriam smiled in affirmation. "Do not overlook the beauty of it all, Matt. The rapid growth, the health of the air, the life burgeoning from the ocean." She turned and a pearl of a tear glistened in the corner of her eye.

REEF MIND

Miriam sighed, and I flinched. I found that I was close to tears myself. "I need to rest." I begged her.

"California is so beautiful. It just needed a boost, is all. That's why I'm here." She took my hand and squeezed it. "I'm so tired, Matt. But don't worry. I'll show you the way."

MATT

MIRIAM'S DEFT HANDS worked to de-bone a fish. My stomach growled, anticipating the meal. I mentioned the unbidden images coming to me, the headaches. Miriam brushed off my concerns. Finally, she spoke over her shoulder at me. "Evolution shaped our brains, making us what we are. We're aware, you see. In a way that goes beyond a basic survival instinct. We cry at sunsets. We look at the vast ocean and find it beautiful, right before the fear sets in."

"You're scared of the ocean?"

"Everyone is. Because we don't want to be alone. Life is so hard and so awful that we can't take it. It doesn't make any sense."

"I never felt like that, not really." I said, squirming in my seated position on a rock. "Before all of this happened, I had a good life. I enjoyed it."

Miriam did not answer. She placed a cast iron pan over the fire, and the smell of the roasting fish made my mouth water. Finally, she remarked, "you're not much for solipsism, are you?"

"I don't even know what that means."

Her white teeth flashed briefly in a smile. "I envy your unburdened mind."

I couldn't tell if she was insulting me or not. I decided she was being honest, because her face didn't flicker with irony or insincerity. I knew I was not well-read. But Miriam seemed to burst with knowledge. "You mean some people hate life. Right?"

She nodded. "It's a kind of pessimism. It is a view that posits that human life is a mistake and we should go extinct."

"Oh. But why? Extinction is bad. We're always upset when certain animal species are endangered. Why kill ourselves?"

REEF MIND

Miriam smiled at me, handing me a plate. "We're bad. Don't you think?"

"Not all of us."

"We're good at making excuses." She amended.

I wonder if you even have a brain. Like what humans understand it to be. When I sawed off your head I felt like I was cutting through a log. You did not react. Your limbs did not spasm. How do you work? Do you think, or is your entire body a shell over one massive nerve cluster, reacting to something larger?

"None of this makes sense. Why would your university send you to La Jolla?" I asked Miriam. "We don't have reefs here. San Diego isn't Australia. Or Hawai'i."

Miriam was busy pulling down a net she'd tied between opposite trees, the calcified branches bone-white. No catch today. Her annoyance was carried in her shoulders.

She said: "You do realize that researchers have only studied less than one percent of California's seafloor?"

"No Miriam, I'm a firefighter."

"I do not think you have the whole picture." She sat down, considering me. "Here is something I know we share, Matt," she explained. "The hitch in our thoughts, the slippage of normal reactions. I found that conversations no longer had common assumptions."

"I don't care about that. I don't want to talk about it, you understand? But you said that California needed you. *Why*?"

She watched me with an expression I could not fully read. "Even now, you resist."

Something was wrong with Miriam. Her story, for one thing. I felt like I knew things about her and didn't, all at once. That unknown was unnerving, like a shadow that would come over her face. I felt saliva flood my mouth. She'd done something. Something bad. But what?

"Can't you even see the beauty of it?" Her voice was tentative. "Watching the coral come back was so beautiful. I approached it with scientific interest, at first. But it was like a siren call. And it reached out to me, Matt. It loves me."

I could feel my stomach tighten, my brain faint with fear. Reubens came to mind for me then, of all people. His distrust of the coral and his despair at the state of the world, now, struck me with an inherent reasonableness. What had happened to Amanda in our apartment was cancerous. Evil. What the fuck was this talk about *love*?

"I can't see the coral as personal, like that. I think that it acts on instinct, like an interconnected organism, but I don't think it speaks to me in a way that makes me relate to it."

Miriam smiled. "You are correct in one sense. No need to anthropomorphize everything; that is hubris. But a flower need not speak. It only blossoms. And it can draw us in with beauty. That is an invitation. It was a call I accepted. I will admit that it was hard at first, but my loved ones were the first to succumb to metamorphosis." She smiled to herself, then. "And when I got here, I was like a midwife. I eased my colleagues into the new reality. What I did for them was an act of love."

My knuckles whitened as I balled my hands into fists. I could feel sweat on my neck. Cold. "Miriam, what did you do?"

Instead of answering, her face took on a dreamy expression. She looked out over her garden and spoke with a sentimental warble in her voice.

"Picture it," she said, spreading her arms out. "The start of all life in the ocean. For them, this land we occupy is a separate world and they are the colonists, the explorers, the first to be in this place. Because of some hiccup, or some instinct, they fell asleep. A long hibernation, or an essential life-cycle action. It doesn't matter. What matters is their perspective. Because they have one, Matt. They are *aware*."

"Imagine thinking the world is a certain way only to wake up to boiling heat and filth and decay. It would be like discovering your hair thriving with lice: lice that soil, consume, and destroy the body. Humans are nasty, naked, squirming. You would exterminate them immediately. You would take drastic action."

I walked closer to the garden as she spoke, her voice firm now, like an orator relating a Homeric passage from memory. I didn't know what I was looking for, but I felt an urgency.

"And yet, Matt, what started as reaction, tempered. Call it a curious interest, or maybe something more noble. A call and response cycle. We must adjust to the fact that we are not the dominant life form. It has always been here. It will do what it needs to. Therefore, wouldn't you rather share life with it? Your understanding of the ecosystem must transcend."

Stony corals brushed against my bare legs, leaving scratches. A few polyps turned in my direction, sensing me in a benign way. I stopped when the rows became a little more unruly, the colorful growths branching out in an upside down "y" pattern. I stopped, my eyes searching, like someone caught at a fork in a path. Miriam walked slowly, circling her garden, eyes still full of fervor.

"Our bodies are capable of much. Our bones can be reinforced by aragonite, once the skin is shucked by the larvae that burrow in. This is the price of blossoming. Your wife stopped eating because she was photosynthesizing, do you understand? She is not really gone. I know you know this. You saw her, or at least, a version of her."

Oh no oh no. The v shape extended up to form a torso, then two arms branched outward. It was an explosion of coral growth in a chalk outline. How had I not seen it . . . ?

"How do you know anything about my wife?"

"I know because she told me. Look at my children, Matt. I am comfortable calling them this, it is the most analogous relationship. I raised them in a nursery, and then took care of them and sheltered them. I planted them in places where I knew they could thrive, and they grew. I pruned them, and then nurtured those clippings in the trailer. They reproduced. I am a mother and now a grandmother."

"You planted them." I whispered.

I lowered myself into a squat. I'd found the head. The skull was obscured in bursts of chromatic growth, but opalescent teeth grinned up at me through the fronds. A garden stake through the mouth anchored it to the ground.

"Miriam," I said, but then I lost my nerve.

"Please, explore the garden, Matt. Listen. We can start small. I will introduce you. That one is soft, and bright pink. You may touch the fronds, which will feel leathery and pliant. Coral has always been part rock, part flower. But now it shares something with us."

My back erupted with pain. A thousand needles stabbed my

skin. Still crouched low, I moved to stand up, but Miriam pushed down on the back of my head. Startled, I toppled forward, over the blooming corpse.

On the other side of the blooming body was your head. The same head I thought I'd left on the stone high, high above this place. This was how Miriam knew me. Miriam had found you and relocated you here, and I felt that truth as certain as the visions that came over me in fits. A call and response cycle, like she'd said. Your eye-sockets were windows into the hollow emptiness of a porcelain doll. But then, a shadow flittered inside, then blinked away. *What the—*

The thing that had grown from your neck detached, its bulbous head ballooning as its snake arms thrashed along the ground. I saw a flash of blotchy blue and black and purple, the thing an animate bruise. One red eye popped open and stopped right in front of my nose as the arms encircled my forearms tight as a vise.

The scream was squeezed out of me, like my lungs were being wrung out. The ground and sky blurred as I panicked, and then Miriam was looking down at me, placid as ever.

"Let's begin."

MATT

THE SLIPPERY ARMS loosened their grip around me slightly, and I gasped.

Their suction cups pulsed against my bare skin in intervals; the veins in my forehead bulged. I looked like I was prostrate in prayer, my head bowed to stare into the bloodshot, sticky eye. The thing's pupil widened so that I looked down into a black mirror. My arms were rooted to the spot. Its tendrils grew branches, small and spidery black veins that painted themselves up my arms. It looked like a giant neuron in shape, the bulbous eye fixed on me, a nucleus of terror.

I could not look away.

Why do I want to obey?

The compulsions I'd felt before were revealed to be nudges, suggestions. This was something more powerful. This was force. There were pinpricks of suction on my skin, from wrist to shoulder. My arms took a chill, deadened like cold fish. *No.* I started to pull away. I felt like I was falling into a deep and dark well full of ancient whispers and knowledge that would swallow me whole.

"Be still!" Miriam hissed behind me.

I complied. All that existed was the eye. My pale and terrified face looked up at me. "W-what is this?" I felt the crotch of my pants warm, then dampen cold. I started to turn my head away from the eye, but an invisible force pressed against my head. My eyeballs hurt, the pressure only letting up when I turned back to the eye.

"If you look away you'll go mad, perhaps die. Do you want to risk that?"

I felt my stomach clench with fear. I considered the parked trailer in my peripheral vision. You were inside. The other you, the body with the newly grown head. I wondered if you cared about me. I wondered if you knew what was happening.

"I'll call for help," I stated in an unconvincing voice.
"If you wish."

A vision formed in the black mirror below me. A face, formed with branchlike villae, which snaked and slithered to form an outline. A jaw. A nose. The recessed holes for my eyes. Miriam said I'd go mad if I looked away. What, then, was this? *This isn't what I want*, I thought. Then it was as if a confluence of whispers in my head adjusted pitch, until I knew the voice.

Any child of ours should have your nose.

Shit. Holy shit, what—

Hot tears blurred my vision. They obscured the image of my wife in the eye. My Amanda. Her lovely voice. I could almost imagine her breath on my ear. Her scent. She was gone and I only had this. And this was a perverse imitation. I'd never feel her skin again. This was it. Gone.

Gone.

Pain. It hurt so badly. The burning sensation on my back was unbearable. The stinging nettle moving and boiling under my skin. The tendrils shivered along my arms. A ripple of offense, I think. Like a lover removing her hand.

You never wanted me anyway, Matt. Not the real me. I was a distraction for you.

Hot shame and despair flooded my body as if my blood were comprised of it. Fuck the coral, how was it doing this? It had a version of Amanda. Not the laughing Amanda at bars or the confident and sexy Amanda surfing an impressive set of waves. This was the Amanda that cried in the bedroom when she didn't think I could hear her. This was the Amanda whose expression faltered when little kids sang songs on their way to school. The Amanda that looked out the window on rainy days with a mug of tea, her eyes glazed over.

We can have a family, Matt.

The flood of memory made my heart swell with so much hurt I was afraid it would break my sternum. Yet, something occurred to me. I couldn't fix this with a good dinner, drinks outside, or nice sex. But maybe, just maybe, I knew how to make it stop hurting me.

With a deep breath I focused, every sense sharp with fear. Breath reduced to clipped gasps, I focused on being let go. I held the gaze of the eye. *Actually, this is what I've always wanted.*

REEF MIND

The skin on my back cooled. The tendrils around my arms did not release me, but they filled like veins rushing with blood. They bulged: soft, tender. Amanda's voice cooed between my ears. Spots swam in my vision as I breathed deeply with relief.

So. It could be lied to. In that way, it was a great deal like Amanda.

I never wanted kids. Not like she did. It had been simple to lie: *I'd have babies with you, honey. But don't dwell on what we can't have.* I let her build up a fantasy of me as some kind of thwarted father figure. That's what it took, sometimes.

I gazed into the eye again. *You're all I want, Amanda. I'll do whatever you need.*

I felt Miriam standing behind me, looking at me. Like every authority figure I've ever had watching me: a parent, a teacher, an inspector. My spine tightened. I felt that Miriam disapproved of me, somehow. Did she know I was lying to this thing? How could she? Could she pick up on insincerity in my body language? In the posture of my spine?

I projected my love for my wife into the eye. Two things happened. The release, and true relief. I fell sideways. The large neuron slithered off my arms. I shook and put my forehead to the ground. Next, a series of sounds: The clink of metal. The squeak of the trailer door opening. Miriam's footsteps on the dirt, coming closer to me. I remembered my father approaching to whip me after I'd run away from him at a garden store.

I tried to sit up, feeling anxious, but my head swam. My stiff arms stung as blood rushed back into them. My vision had the haze of someone recently sick. A blurred edge, a suggestion of unreality. Miriam had tools. Rope, large garden stakes. She set down the rope. Weighed the stake in her hand, then looked at me. A flicker of panic rose in my hollow belly.

I'd already had an inkling of what she would do to me. My eyes shifted sideways to confront a skeletal rictus that crawled with algae. It was taunting me: *you're fucked, buddy.*

And then it all happened so fast. You were standing behind her, your arm raised. The sunlight shone through your head, a ruby red star. Your hand was a shadow passing by the sun, making the light blink, and then Miriam fell. Her body landed with a soft thud. Still trembling, I managed to sit up, confused.

HAZEL ZORN

You bent over Miriam and pushed a stake further down into the ground. Her limbs convulsed.

You'd stabbed her. Through her left breast.

It was all so quiet.

You walked over to me, dropped into a low squat. I recoiled, too tired to run. My throat was raw. I felt close to tears.

The creature on the ground twitched. The neuron-shape slithered across the ground, and then its tendrils were sliding up my back, wrapping around my shoulders, under my armpits. Somehow tangible yet intangible, like a shadow cast over me before becoming more solid. It rested against my spine, a gentle heartbeat that regulated itself to my own body's rhythms. You watched this. And then you held up a large shirt with a logo that read MARINE RESTORATION over the right breast pocket.

I put it on, and the thing on my back purred. Fingers slipped into the wrinkled matter of my mind. Gentle.

It's ok, baby. You've always been my hero. My fireman.

My body stopped trembling. I stood up.

Miriam's body was decomposing. Psychedelic moss grew in hairy patches over her chest and arms. This thing on me was connected to the reef mind, and Miriam had been serving it. For some reason it had chosen me over her.

Miriam's eyes glazed over. Her head lolled upright to look blankly at the clouds.

"Strange," she gurgled. Blood bubbles foamed across her lips. "It's silent. It's so *quiet—*"

MATT

STOOD AT the edge of the mesa and looked out over the Mojave Desert. The approaching dusk dotted the sky with stars as we traversed the Providence Mountain area. A sign for tourists had been knocked to the ground. I munched on a piece of jerky, my mouth dry. I'd wrapped an oversized shirt around my head. My beard had grown to cover my neck. You, beside me, pulled back your own head covering and smelled the air. The redness of your face had yielded to a milky flesh color over the length of five days. Your eyes remained pink.

Amanda loved you. I felt her love course through my own heart.

I'd spent the latter half of my life chasing a vision of myself as the noble hero. Amanda knew this about me. She'd placed a mission on my heart, one that I could not imagine refusing. Together, you and I planted coral clippings where growth was sparse, by the Joshua trees and runoffs where underground rivers made small oases in the barren sand.

You're wonderful, Matt. This is exactly what I need. Amanda guided me with subtle twitches and suggestions, one neuron in an interlinked system that guided the coral with intelligence. I had flashes of insight—communication, I knew, between the various reefpoints all over the world. It was a pleasure point, these visions: a purr on my back, which led to an exciting ripple along my flesh that culminated between my legs.

They were all in the ocean, their reach thinning out further inland. Coral growth that found purchase further from the water grew wild and erratically, as if too far from their master commander to act strategically. I was aware of these facts the way anyone is aware of the existence of geographical places they've never visited.

HAZEL ZORN

We had to find an ideal body of water. Amanda and I would make a home there. You, I noticed, could no longer walk on the air as we traversed onward. You were becoming more solid. Fleshy. We had to make sure you were at home in this world.

It was what Amanda wanted.

We kicked up dust on our way down an arroyo, and the clatter of loose rock gave away our position to a rider. A pony with a tired trot, the rider wrapped in a shroud. I put up my arms. "Hello, friend!"

The rider halted before us. In the setting sun, we could only make out her shape at first, details clarifying as we walked up to her. It was an old sister; what I thought was a shroud was her habit. Her wrinkled skin was tanned to the color of leather in the hot sun. The pony was saddled with huge goat-skin water bags. The woman bowed her covered head. She greeted us in Spanish, and then switched to English when she heard my accent.

"Hello pilgrim. I wish to pass in peace."

"We aren't bandits," I reassured her. "My daughter and I are travelers."

A flash, then—a quickening feeling, my pants tight. I placed my hands over my belt to hide it. *Ask about lake Havasu.*

"You are about two days away on foot." Was the sister's answer. "You must turn south." Her eyes shone like black beetles. "It is getting dark. We will not refuse you hospitality, but we ask that you move on after a few days."

I was able to voice reassurances. I still needed sleep, though less of it. Our guide was called Sister González, who happened to be part of a teaching order that had fled a city and settled in a camp around fire bunkers in the desert. There were several dozen of them left, all from Mexico. Their convent had come to visit a sister house in California when the crisis hit. She mentioned their mission, the details of which became clearer as we approached. Nearer to the camp we heard the voices of children, the loud and playful screaming often characteristic of playgrounds.

The fire bunkers were large, circular structures made of concrete. They were accessed via a hatch door, and descended underground. They made the children sleep inside for the night.

REEF MIND

This was to "ward off the voices" that called in the late hours, and to protect them from "contamination."

Several sisters were about and working as we entered the encampment. All wore the same practical habit: navy blue, with a head covering that only went to the shoulders, a billowing linen top and skirt, and leather sandals. Some were teaching, others minding smaller toddlers. There was an infant being rocked to sleep.

The old woman dismounted and led us to a small stable, where her pony threw its head up a few times in agitation. Sister González bent low to look at a suspicious growth near a cactus. Soft coral growth, I realized. Easy to miss in the mess of thorny cacti.

There were pale limestone faces in their center. They looked childlike, sculpted cheeks and rose-petal lips, eyes closed peacefully. You were looking at them, as if entranced. You reached out your hand, but the sister grabbed your elbow.

"Don't listen! They harvest memories of your loved ones. They are liars."

"What's that?" I was surprised into asking.

The old woman shook her head. "Do not underestimate its intelligence."

Curious, and a bit agitated, I forced my voice into a neutral tone. "How do you know it's intelligent?"

"Because it is perverse."

Morning came, and my stomach roiled with my passenger's unease. I did not realize why until I saw a line of fire burning in the distance. You cowered at the sight of it. "Don't worry, it won't reach us." I squinted, realizing something. No wind, perfect humidity levels. "That's a controlled burn."

Breakfast was a thin gruel from a communal pot. Sister González overheard me and admitted that they were setting small fires to deter coral growth in the area. "You can give us tips then," she half-joked. "We have noticed that fire clears out any aberrant coral growth. We enforce a perimeter. But this desert is fragile. Fire hurts the plants and animals. It is not like a forest with excess vegetation."

I felt a twitch of panic. "This area is vulnerable to wildfires. Don't you think you're being reckless?"

"Maybe that's why the coral can't get a foothold all the way out here." She replied.

"Neither did humanity. Nobody lives out here, and for good reason." I put my palms on my knees. "I'd never advise a controlled burn out here. You're going to lose control. That's my tip."

Sister didn't answer. I stared out across the rocky, dusty landscape. The mountain peaks crowded out the skyline. A school of fish, too far out to snare, shimmered. "There aren't many fish this far out?"

"Yes! As I said, much of the infection has not spread this far, ¡Gloria a Dios! Now, would you like a second helping?" Her ladle hovered over my bowl, waiting for my answer.

I felt anger throbbing on my back.

AMANDA

WHAT IS CREATION but a terrible cancer haunted by inevitable decay? Human beings were not wrong to multiply. To dominate. They're good at it. But they're more than that. Consciousness made them capable of malice. Pride. Every other animal on the earth just *lives*. They eat to survive and reproduce and if they disappear nothing mourns them.

Does any other creature reproduce out of a sense of superiority?

Consciousness as virus. How interesting. If it's an accident, maybe it's something we caught.

Matt is a linear man. He is human. But that also means that he is predictable. A known quantity. And he will be folded in, absorbed, used. He will deposit us in the lake. He will sink down and become the foundation of a new reef. His bones will flourish. He will be with me.

MATT

"**YOU KNOW,** I think that life is just fine. In fact, I think it's good." My vision burns and blurs as I speak. I feel embarrassed to cry in front of Sister González. She gives me a curious look, a half-smile acknowledging that I've spoken, but no indication that she understands. Perhaps her English is not as good as I thought. Or, more likely, since she is not privy to my internal hauntings, this statement makes no sense. But she is kind. I wipe my eyes, try again. "I have to go now, and I'm sorry."

"We all have our paths." The old woman smiles again. She hands me a refilled canteen.

This is just as well. I could never tell her my real purpose, what I must do. For some reason I do not want to disappoint someone so harmless and good.

"We will be alright." She nods to the east, where the fire is still going.

The thing about fire is that it cannot really be controlled. The encampment is in danger. They should evacuate. I know because of the wind shift, the rise in temperature. All warning signs. I see that the conflagration has already spread to dry grasses. Wildfire is greedy and it always wants more. They must be put out with coordinated teams of airplanes and ground workers.

Something like this, it would take days to fight.

But that isn't me, anymore. I am forced to serve another purpose.

I trace a map to Lake Havasu in the sand with her, confirming my path. The water bisects California and Arizona. South from here, an easy path if I go slowly, and carefully. I close my eyes and see the way to the water. My passenger's excitement, which then turns into my own. My body sinking below the water, filling my ears. Filling me with silence. And solace.

REEF MIND

And then I see a scene through a mask, the eyeholes fitting over my own. La Jolla. Windansea beach, a distant shore. Nobody's around. The salt of the sea splashes onto Miriam's lips, and I taste it. A briny kiss. She's ecstatic. Hand between her legs, rocking back and forth with the motion of the water. Her nipples harden, push against the fabric of her loose shirt. With a groan a starfish-shape births itself from her back, slides down into the boat. Miriam gently puts it into a cooler, and she coos over it. Pets it. Shuts it away from the sun.

Children cannot be fully possessed, nor fully protected. Miriam's heart breaks with my own. She sees the surfers. She lets her baby go into the water. The coral reef mind, one neuron at a time, the blood of her grandfather used as substrate. That's my path. But there are no surfers here in the desert, so my bones will become the foundation of this particular reefpoint.

When I come to, I am disoriented by your presence, sitting beside me.

It's time to go.

I put my hand on your rock-hard shoulder. You almost fit in with the sisters, in your long robe and head covering. They think you're warding off the sun, instead of hiding. Your salmon-pink eyes hold something behind them. Concern? Not for me, surely.

I am talking to you because this is what a man does at the end of his life. Perhaps I am too young to be considered old by human standards. Perhaps I am grasping for relevance.

All I know is that the passage of time presses against me, and it is no longer spring. By now you know that humans can be very bad, but we can also be very good. I admit, I wonder about your inclinations. I have come to see you as an individual. Forgive me for sounding sentimental. I know you don't speak, but we're connected by this monolithic thing. I have to believe you're hearing me.

I never wanted a child. Not with Amanda, not with anyone. I wanted to live for other things. Why be a father to a specific child when I could rescue countless children in need? Maybe my motivations for firefighting weren't *noble*, but I didn't think they were *bad*, either. I knew my talents. I wanted to be respected for them.

I see now that the coral has manipulated that to its own cause. But it made a mistake with me. Well, I think *you* did, to be exact.

I'll let this question linger, because I do not expect an answer: Were you supposed to kill Miriam?

You and I are alone as the sun sets over the desert, and the fire rises in the east. It's out of control now. I see its path when I assess the direction of the wind. I know exactly where a survivor ought to walk, and quick, if they had a mind to be one.

"Don't wait for me," I say to you as I walk away. You do not grab my hand and ask me to stay. You do not beg to go along, either: *daddy let me come with you, please pleaseplease.* You have never been much of a child in any way. We will have no memories of vacationing together, of owning pets, or visiting zoos and playgrounds. There will be no first day of school. Our entire relationship is a graveyard of what was supposed to be.

The fire makes my skin weep with sweat. Its brightness washes out the sky, obscuring even the stars. The smell of burning shrub and dry grass fills my nostrils. A cactus with a polyp infestation hisses and pops to my right. Unable to escape, unable to incorporate the cactus into itself. My back writhes; my passenger lurches in fear.

"It's alright, honey," I find myself saying to it. My face is bubbling with new boils in the heat. The fire encircles me. I am standing in the eye of a storm.

I whisper: "You're not alone."

You will feel what all children are fated to. Your parent shrinks as you grow to meet their eyes. You'll find that many excuses for them don't work anymore. How strange, that cycle of delusion.

But you. Did you ever really know me?

Can you?

NO ONE

HERE WE ARE, here Matt was, here this vessel now walks alone. If that is the correct signifier. What is "together" but many alone in one setting? From here, anything could happen to us. The religious sisters have noticed that we, or *she*, as they call us, does not sweat. We do not make water. There are so many small things we have not mastered. Perhaps we are discovered.

We thought we could manage to convince everyone to accept us as human. We have grown attached to our parentage, after all, and that is an observed human trait. The proximity to Matt especially has influenced our feeling of wholeness. Matt was company the way our algae growths within us, sustaining this vessel, are not.

We were hungry in the dark fire bunker. No sun, no food. We were afraid of algae death. They pulsed within us, feeling up inside the hollows of our arms and legs, never revealing themselves. But we were more afraid of the fire. We lasted several days. When the hatch door finally opened, the air was thick and the sky painted muddy yellow.

The sisters are all saying to us this word: "sorry." For the ash on the wind. For the water rations. For the crying infant, face streaked with soot. One sister found the remains of half of a skull in the hills, and again, the word "sorry."

But Matt was not sorry, at all.

Here is why we ponder the many possibilities. We thought we were one step ahead of this species. We know that Matt's skin curled and peeled away, that cooked fat dribbled yellow from his body, that several of his teeth exploded like popping kernels. He was laughing. Even when his vocal cords melted into his throat and the bloody sludge vomited down his chest. From his back struggled our charge, limbs long and whiplike, trying to peel off.

REEF MIND

Matt grabbed ahold of the tentacles, held tightly until it curled inward and stopped moving. For a while we heard some of his thoughts, all scrambled, only going silent after the fire subsided. Nothing useful. Nothing we can learn from. Many words, no meaning.

In the twilight the sisters sing bedtime songs to children. They call for their mothers, their fathers. Our vessel holds what is left of a skull. Studies it. The caved in eye socket, the charred forehead.

We push the tongue to part the lips. "Da." We flex it against the roof of the mouth. "Da."

We are alive.

We are well.

But we are *wrong*, somehow.

What are we supposed to do with this?

ACKNOWLEDGMENTS

This book is about climate change anxiety. When the world suffers, we suffer. Our collective response is always in flux, but I believe in humanity. Consider donating to a coral restoration fund: **coralgardeners.org**

Thank you to my family near La Jolla, and for the memory of hiking Torrey Pines. This work is my tribute to a truly beautiful place. You can't lose what you don't fully appreciate.

I feel as if every writer collects a cadre of total misfits (other writers, of course) to encourage their insanity. Thank you to Susan, Alec, and Alayna, my first readers. You all didn't know what you were getting into when you met me at the library!

Thank you to my children, for thinking that this book is cool. None of you are allowed to read it until you're twenty. Thank you to my husband, who only watches horror movies with me because I like them. I'm comforted, knowing that I face the uncertainty of the world with you.

ABOUT THE CONTRIBUTORS

Hazel Zorn works as an artist in the Northeastern United States. Visit hazelzorn.com for more.

Becca Snow is an illustrator and bookbinder based in Arizona with a BFA in Drawing from Arizona State University. They enjoy designing book covers and posters with dramatic lighting, colors, and atmosphere, as well as illustrating scenes from their favorite books, shows, and podcasts. They love drawing monsters and spooky things, as well as trying to capture abstract concepts in various art forms, including artist books and pastel paintings.

Echo Echo is a Portuguese artist and a proponent of *horror vacui*. She immerses herself in individual pieces for up to a year at a time and renders in extreme detail. Echo also performs in multiple bands, finding equal freedom in expressing herself through music as she does through illustration.

CONTENT WARNINGS

Being a work of mature Horror, a degree of violence, gore, sex and/or death is to be expected.

In addition, **REEF MIND** contains scenes of pregnancy miscarriage (discussed) and child abuse.

Please be advised.

More information at
www.tenebrouspress.com

Grab another Tenebrous title!

Grab another Tenebrous title!

TENEBROUS PRESS

Home of New Weird Horror, New Weird Dark Fiction, Oddities, Abnormalities and All Manner of Eccentricities You Never Knew You Needed More Than Oxygen

FIND OUT MORE:

www.tenebrouspress.com

@TenebrousPress on social media

HAIL THE TENEBROUS CULT

www.ingramcontent.com/pod-product-compliance
Lightning Source LLC
LaVergne TN
LVHW092045290625
814921LV00003B/100